What the critics are saying…

5 Stars! *"Ms. Dane's* debut novel is absolutely fabulous! *Ms. Dane* demonstrates how extremely creative she is by enrapturing her fans with exciting and deliciously appealing characters which she weaves into the most beautifully sensual love scenes" ~ *Di Nogueras Ecataromance*

5 Flags! "*Lauren Dane* has created a wonderful story filled with witches, vampires, wizards, demons, angels and demigods.(…)Be advised, you will find yourself pursuing this author for a return trip to the witches o*f New Orleans.* Let's hope that she complies quickly because Triad was just too good to leave so quickly." ~ *Raashema Euro-Reviews*

5 Angels and A Recommended Read! "Welcome to *Lauren Dane's Triad,* a fantastic world of witches, wizards, vampires and demons, full of love, passion, magic and suspense. This thriller will hook you from beginning to the end. Triad is a scorching hot, pager-turner with a marvelous, suspenseful plot that kept me tied up in knots until the very end.(…) I am proud to grant Triad with 5 scorching Angels and a Recommended Read." ~ *Contessa. Fallen Angels*

5 Roses! "A spectacular debut for author Lauren Dane! Triad weaves a spell on you right from the start with its vivid detail and dynamic characters. You can almost feel the moist heat of New Orleans seeping into your soul" ~ *Cynthia A Romance Review*

TRIAD

Lauren Dane

ELLORA'S CAVE
ROMANTICA PUBLISHING

An Ellora's Cave Romantica Publication

www.ellorascave.com

Triad

ISBN # 1419952900
ALL RIGHTS RESERVED.
Triad Copyright© 2005 Lauren Dane
Edited by: Ann Leveille
Cover art by: Syneca

Electronic book Publication: May, 2005
Trade paperback Publication: November, 2005

Excerpt from *Stephanie Menage* Copyright © Mari Byrne, 2003

Warning:

Triad

Dedication

Thank you Ray, for believing in me and being the best thing that's ever happened to me. Mom and Dad, thanks so much for always encouraging my creativity and for being my number one fans. Last, but never least, thank you to my superheroine editor, Ann—you're a great editor and you've made me a better writer.

Chapter One

Amelia Charvez sat in the window seat of her New Orleans apartment and looked out over the courtyard below. The sounds of the water gurgling in the fountain floated up on the wind. She breathed deeply and took a sip of the red wine that her sister Emily had brought by earlier in the day.

"Lee, come in here and tell me what you think of this sauce," Em called out to her from the kitchen.

Lee stood up and sauntered into the kitchen and tasted the sauce for the redfish her sister was making them for dinner. "More garlic and black pepper, I think," she murmured.

"What's going on with you?" Em asked as she tossed in another clove of garlic and ground some pepper over the pan. "You seem distracted."

"I am. There's something up, something on the wind. I've been dreaming a lot."

"The tall, golden-haired man again?"

"Yeah." Lee shivered at the mention of the man who'd been haunting her dreams for the last two months straight.

"You need to have a reading. This sauce is gonna have to simmer for another half an hour anyway, go down to the shop and have *tante* Lou give you one. Go on. I've never seen you so distracted before."

Lee started to argue but shrugged her shoulders, giving in to her sister's suggestion. "Why not?" She put on her sandals and ran her fingers through her hair to try to tame the curly mass. "I'll be back," she called out as she walked out and down the steps into the lushly appointed courtyard. She breathed deeply of the sweet greenery and pushed through the black iron gate that led out to the street.

Lee walked from her apartment on the edge of the quarter the several blocks until she emerged into the heart of the French Quarter, with its music and magic in the air. She walked two more blocks to her grandmother's shop and went inside, feeling calmer immediately as the scent of incense hit her nose and the familiar surroundings came into view.

"Sugar! I knew you was coming in! You need a reading, yeah?" her *tante* Lou called out as Lee walked through the black velvet curtains that separated the shop from where her aunt held readings in the back.

"You must be psychic," Lee joked and grinned at her aunt and dropped a kiss to her cheek. She sat down on the small loveseat, tucking her feet beneath her bottom.

Tante Lou took her hand and ran her thumbs over the palm gently, soothing her. "You been dreaming, yeah?" she asked, eyes closed. "Sug, you are facing some big changes. A man, golden-haired and powerful, he comes. He is part of you." Lou was quiet for a bit, breathing slowly. Lee waited patiently for her aunt to continue. "But that does not complete the circuit."

She opened her eyes and looked at Lee. "Lee, honey, this man, he is nothing to fear. But you do have some powerful things to face, some of them dark, very dark. I can't see a whole lot, watch yourself. Practice. You have a lot of power, you simply need to hone it, to use it. You know we've been feeling some rather disturbing energy lately. The energy your *grandmere* and I have been feeling is dark and cold. Threatening. You'll need to watch out."

Lee knew this, she'd had her dreams and also some conversations with her *grandmere* about it. New Orleans was a hotbed of magic, which made it a great place for her to be but it was a dangerous thing as well. There was so much old and powerful magic there, just waiting to be tapped into, it often attracted those who were less than responsible with it.

"So to cap up, I'm gonna meet a guy who is my other half and that's good, but there is some supernatural shit coming down the pike?" Lee asked bluntly.

"Not your other half exactly." *Tante* Lou hesitated, reaching for the proper words. "He is part of you, you are part of him and you are meant to be with each other. But there's more, I can't say what. It is good though. The other, yes, bad doodoo."

Lee laughed and kissed her aunt's cheek and got up and went back out front. She greeted her cousin, grabbing a pack of spring rain incense and some tea, dropped money on the counter, and headed home.

* * * * *

After dinner with her sister, Lee sat in her window seat and stared out into the night. This dark power on the horizon posed a big threat to them all and she knew she had a responsibility to deal with it. Her power didn't come for free, she knew that as an inherent witch, she had a duty to use her gifts to protect those who needed them. Problem was, she knew what she had to do and it entailed swallowing her pride and calling her mother and restarting the training she'd set aside years before. It wasn't like she'd totally rejected her power, she did small magics from time to time, she knew she had the raw power. She needed help in using it effectively. Sighing resignedly, she picked up the phone and called home.

"*Maman*?"

"I've been waiting for you to call, *cher*. Tomorrow, eleven o'clock. Come out to the house, we will start. Lock your doors. *Je t'aime*," her mother said, sounding imperious, and hung up.

Lee looked at the phone and with a wry smile, hung up and checked the locks and went to bed. Her mother was a no-nonsense woman and a very no-nonsense witch. The women in the Charvez family were born with magical gifts. Some, like *tante* Lou and her *grandmere*, could read the future. Some, like her sister Emily and her cousin, could read people, their intentions, their wants, hopes, dreams. And the most powerful and rare of all were the witch dreamers.

A witch dreamer was able to work magic both awake and in her dreams. They also had a touch of clairvoyance, could see snatches of future events occurring as waking dreams or while unconscious. The witch dreamer could dream walk, she could project herself into the subconscious of others and work her magic there. There were only three living witch dreamers, it was an exceptionally rare gift. It seemed to be singular to the Charvez women—Lee, her mother and her great-aunt Elise—just one woman a generation.

Lee had accepted that but hadn't done a whole lot to hone her power. Against her family's wishes she'd gone off to college at Tulane, refusing to believe that she had only one path for her life. As conciliation to the family, she'd planned to go to graduate school, to get her MBA so she could help run the shop, but she'd gotten distracted. Distracted by art, something she never thought she'd have the talent for. But now, two years later, she'd built up a steady customer base and two shops on Royal Street had her paintings in the front windows. It was a good living, enough to pay her rent and allow for a nest egg, and she could still do her part in the running of the shop.

* * * * *

Lee thought about all of this on her way over to her parents' home. Thought about her responsibility, the legacy of the Charvez magic. And she realized that she had a lot to learn, a lot to be taught and she felt a twinge of guilt for waiting so long to truly figure that out.

Still, all of that worry fell away when she caught sight of the house. The house on First Street was the house Lee grew up in, the place she and her siblings were born. Before that, her grandparents had lived there. It generally passed down from oldest daughter to oldest daughter and would be hers someday but she had no plans to kick her parents out, she quite enjoyed the privacy of her two-bedroom apartment in the French Quarter.

She loved her mother but it was easier to love her from a bit of a distance.

She breathed deeply and took in the heady smells of New Orleans in the early summer. It was hot and moist and burgeoning with the heady, fecund scent of flowers and trees, grass and dirt. Nature was tangible, it hung in the air. As always, there was the underlying scent of power and death from Lafayette Cemetery just a few blocks away. No place on earth smelled as heavenly, as magical and heady, as New Orleans did.

Lee parked in the driveway and walked around the back and in through the kitchen. She called out a greeting and kissed Georgie, the woman who managed the household and had since before Lee was born. Georgie was a cook, a maid, a social planner and a member of the family. She murmured her greetings to Lee and stuffed a plum into her hand. "Eat it, girl, you getting too skinny."

Lee smiled wryly and bit into the juicy plum and her eyes slid shut at the pleasure of the sweet juice bursting over her tongue and sliding down her throat. "Oh good lord, this is so good."

"Off my tree. Stop by before you go, I'll make sure you get a few jars of my jam and one of the tarts I made this morning."

"You are too good to me," Lee said with a grin.

"Your mama is in the front room. She's waiting for you."

Lee winked at Georgie and walked through after tossing the plum pit into the trash and wiping off her hands and chin. The house was cool and calm as she walked through to the front room where she saw her mother sitting in a wingback chair near the windows overlooking the front lawn and garden.

She bent and kissed her mother's cheeks and flopped on the floor at her feet and rested her head on her mother's knees. Her relationship with her mother had always been complicated. Marie Charvez was a powerful woman, a powerful witch, and she knew that her daughter was as well. She took a great deal of pride from the fact that she'd birthed a witch dreamer with so much potential and she'd pushed Lee hard for most of her young life. So hard that at times Lee felt more like a project than a daughter.

Things had come to a head when Lee had decided to go off to college rather than pursue her training. She and her mother hadn't spoken for nearly six months and it had been the most difficult time of her life. Slowly, with the steadfast urging of her father and *tante* Elise, she and her mother had come back together with a better understanding of each other. Years later, Lee felt that the time spent apart and then struggling to meet each other as mother and daughter had made them closer than they would have been had she stayed and been obedient to her mother's master plan.

"Good morning, *maman*."

"Good morning, *cher*. You look lovely today. The humidity is making your hair curl up even more than it usually does. You look wild and tousled," her mother said quietly, with amusement in her voice. She sat up, her tone turning businesslike. "You will come to me, each day at eleven. We have a lot of work to do. I feel something in the air. I've been dreaming a lot. Something powerful is…" she broke off, trying to define what she meant.

"Surging. No, surfacing," Lee said hesitantly, searching for the right words to describe what she'd been feeling.

"Yes. As always, there are currents of power here. We all recognize each other, the white path is stronger than the dark one but we keep to our places and behave, it is the order of things. Lately, the dark, it is rising, yes, surfacing is a good enough word. You must work to harness your power. I've spent a lot of energy over the last ten years, shielding you from things. I cannot any longer. Your power is like a spotlight, Lee, it is blinding, it attracts the eye. You are the strongest of us in generations but you must learn to handle it, to wield it. I fear that you will *have* to."

Lee felt a frisson of fear but a certainty that her mother was right. "Okay. I'll be here."

"Let's get started. You know rudimentary spells, the basics. What I want to do is show you how to unleash your power, to slowly let out the reins and then harness it and reel it back in. It's a lot like making you play scales, yes? Necessary. You need to feel your power under your hands, you need to feel it so you can learn to manipulate it, how to control it, how to unleash it."

Her mother pulled the curtains closed and lit some incense. "You know it isn't necessary to do all of this, your power is there without ritual, but it's nice to give a bit of respect to it when you can," she said in her rich melodic tones. "I want you to draw a circle of protection around us, always use one if you have the time. When your power has been dormant for so long and you unleash it you will attract some — how do you say? — onlookers. Most are harmless but never forget where you are, *cher*." Her mother handed her the pouch of sand and watched while Lee said the words and drew a circle around them. Lee felt the hair on her arms raise and a chill run down her spine as she closed it and her mother looked at her, eyebrows raised.

Lee sat down cross-legged before her mother and listened carefully to her instructions. She exhaled slowly and sank into herself, pulling away the shields she normally had up between her power and her daily life. She reached down and connected with her power, with the earth, and felt it surge up, her soul would be the conduit. An electric hum filled her ears and subsided as she let the power roll over her, through her. She reached down and grasped the energy and pulled it out of herself. It flooded out, wave after wave until she felt as if she were floating in it. She opened her eyes and saw her mother's face, eyes wide, and realized she *was* floating in it. She was about half a foot off the ground.

"Cast yourself out, Lee, I want you to sense what's going on around you. Leave this house on your power."

Lee let go of her metaphysical self and it poured out through the house, where she saw Georgie in the kitchen, humming, wearing an amulet of protection, then out of the house and through the neighborhood. She touched some other spots of power, nothing overwhelming. Minor psychics, though many of them probably didn't even know it. She edged around the cemetery and saw more clearly the things she felt as she passed through normally. There were dark spots, someone was practicing some dark magic, there were light spots there too. The place was a city of the dead but it was also a place of power.

As she flowed outward she felt a tugging. Lee focused on it but it felt sticky like a spider web. Alarmed, she circled back and headed back into herself, reining her power back in. As she did she felt a presence, someone was watching her. Some*thing* was watching her. It chilled her. She felt like someone was taking her measure, examining her. Instinctively, she lashed out at it and sent it reeling. She came back to herself and saw her mother's worried face.

"What was that?" Lee asked in a whisper.

Her mother held up a hand to silence her. Her lips were moving. She was working a spell. A dark shadow fell over the house. Lee's hands joined with her mother's and she lent her mother power. She felt her mother pull it into herself and felt it build as she continued with the words. Lee could feel the presence of something truly evil, dark and malevolent. Its manifestation was like oil, sticky and toxic. She sent more power to her mother and at the same time lashed out at the encroaching presence like a whip. She felt her power strike the dark power and only just kept herself from recoiling in repulsion as her power touched the darkness. But it was enough and the malevolence receded.

Moments later her mother's eyes opened and she looked at Lee, worried. "We held it off." *This time* was the unspoken end of the sentence.

"What was it?"

"I've felt a lot of black magic in my life, but I haven't felt anything remotely like this since I was very young and my *tante* Elise was training me. It knows you now, it knows me. I'm going to call *tante* Elise and have her help you ward your apartment and re-ward the shop and this house. We must be vigilant, and,

Lee, you must continue to train because I fear you will have to deal with this, whatever it is."

Her mother looked toward the door where just down the hall they could hear Georgie working and she looked back to Lee. "Perhaps we shouldn't train here. Georgie's amulet might work for run-of-the-mill dark magic but what I felt earlier, I was glad to be in the circle. We can't count on the source of this power to obey the rules about innocents."

Lee shuddered at the idea of their friend being harmed. "You're right. We can train in the shop. It would be better anyway to have that many powerful women close at hand."

They worked on some protection spells for another few hours and enjoyed some tea and gossip in the kitchen. Lee felt a bit better armed when she got up to leave. "I need to go. *Tante* Elise is meeting me at my apartment in a bit to help with the wards. I'll see you at the shop tomorrow." Lee bent to kiss her mother and Georgie and left them both, still sitting at the table, drinking sweet tea.

* * * * *

Her *tante* Elise was waiting for her, sitting on the stone bench in the courtyard. She was looking down at the wool in her hands, knitting like a fiend, her still-dark hair held back in the neat bun she habitually wore at the back of her head. The birds had clustered close by. It had been like that for as long as Lee could remember. *Tante* Elise called to the wild things wherever she went. Birds, butterflies, dogs, cats, whatever was around.

Smiling, Lee went to the older woman and hugged her, kissing her cheeks. She unlocked the door, but before she could step inside *Tante* Elise held out a hand to stop her, shaking her head. "Feel it, *cher*. Go in first and feel it, make sure there are no dark spots, yes?"

Lee nodded and quickly let down her shielding. She sent her power into her apartment, rolling it through the rooms, feeling for any traps or problems. She discovered a small dark spot and, puzzled, she turned to her great-aunt who nodded and said, "Get rid of it."

Lee reached out with her power and grabbed that dark spot. She surrounded it with light, balled it up and it dissipated. She felt *tante* Elise's power come in behind her and sweep through. The apartment felt better, cleaner. She came back to herself and *tante* Elise nodded and they went inside, closing the door behind them.

"What was that?" Lee asked.

"Something dark has been here, not very long because it was just a small spot. You got rid of it, I can't feel anything else. You did well."

"Something evil was in my apartment?" She was creeped out. Lee pulled out a chair for her great-aunt to sit in.

Tante Elise looked at Lee critically. "I can see that we've waited long enough to talk to you about all of the things you need to know," she said nodding decisively. "Lee, I fear that you have never really been impressed with just how powerful you are. Oh, sure you know you are a witch dreamer and therefore have power, but you don't understand the depth of it.

"Your *grandmere* and I wanted you to have a bit of time to find your way back to us, to accept who you are and she was right of course, that if pressed you would have balked and now that you are accepting, you are growing by lengths. Think of your power, of all power, like lights in the dark. They attract attention, bugs and other things wish to cluster 'round. The light brightens the way through the darkness. It's warm, inviting. But there are darker things out there than the feeble little dark magic practitioners who wish to hurl curses and illness, these darker things feed on the light, on the power that others have. The more power, the more attractive."

Lee went to grab something cool to drink for her and *tante* Elise sighed and nodded in appreciation when Lee set a cool glass of tea before her and set the air conditioner and ceiling fans. "Charvez women are strong, you know this. Be they healers or seers or readers or, like you and me and your *maman*, witch dreamers. We have always been an attraction to the less than wholesome things in this world. Mainly we have been left alone because we are so powerful, especially as a unit. But this time is different. While our power as a family is important, your power as a witch dreamer is the key here."

Lee looked at her with surprise but *tante* Elise held her hand up to command silence and continued.

"*Cher*, from the moment you were born, I knew you were the most powerful witch our family has seen since my great-grandmother was a child. Seven generations ago was the last time we saw power such as yours. I felt you today, I expect all who have any kind of power felt you today. You unfurled the total extent of your power for the first time ever and you rode it. But even before you released it, when it was shielded and bottled up, it was still there. Your mother has done her best to screen you from onlookers, but it can't be totally hidden."

Tante Elise exhaled slowly. "I fear that something truly dark, something truly malevolent, is out there in New Orleans right now. It is only awakening but it knows you, it knows us and you must train to meet and vanquish it. I know, it sounds melodramatic but there it is. With power comes responsibility. The Charvez women have served to protect the innocents for generations and that's our job, *your* job."

"Our job? So I'm like the chosen one or something?" Lee responded glibly.

Tante Elise laughed and patted her arm. "You aren't quite as fashionable. But in a way, yes. You won't fight vampires every night and face the end of the world at the end of every May, but we have a pact of sorts, a compact, which charges us with the protection of innocents here in the area. It was made a very long time ago to protect ourselves, to protect our neighbors from evil. It's worked."

"A pact? With who? What about? How come I didn't know about this?"

"I expect that your *maman* felt that it wasn't time yet. Each witch dreamer is told when she is able to take up the mantle of power from the last. Your *maman* was in her late twenties when I judged her ready."

Lee was reeling from all that she was hearing.

Tante Elise took a drink of her tea and continued. "You know of course that the Charvez women are all born with gifts. It has been this way for generations. In 1773 Annalisa Charvez was a witch—" *Tante* Elise shrugged her shoulders, " —not unusual, of course, for us. She was a healer. She delivered the babies, healed toothaches, made tinctures and tonics for the locals. They trusted her to protect their health.

"She was coming back to her house after being out at a shack in the middle of the swamps for two days delivering a baby. She stumbled upon a being of light under attack from a being of darkness. Annalisa intervened, and using her powers combined with those of the other creature, they conquered the creature of the dark, a demon lord, and saved the angel.

"When the angel gained the upper hand with the demon it created the Compact. Until the extinction of the Charvez line, each generation of girl children would be born with gifts to protect the people of whatever area they inhabited. One of those girl children per generation, and only one of them, would be their chief protector, a witch who could wield her magic in both waking hours and while asleep. The demon did not wish to agree but it was trapped, and the angel used that to force an accord and the Compact was born."

Tante Elise reached out and grasped both of Lee's hands. "You are the protector of this generation, Lee. It is your job, your sworn obligation to use your power to defend the innocents here in New Orleans. It is a heavy mantle to carry but I have faith in you, Lee. I have faith in your strength, your loyalty and your power. You will beat whatever this is. And it has to be you. A witch dreamer was the first to defeat the demon, it has to be the same now."

Lee stared at her great-aunt, dumbfounded and a bit awestruck. "So uh, I'm like a superhero? Do I quit my day job and superhero full time now?"

Tante Elise laughed. "Your life won't change for the most part. You'll continue to paint and to work at the shop and to be the vibrant woman you are, you'll just have another facet, that's all."

"Another facet?" She'd run from it for a long time, the truth was that the afternoon had left her feeling energized, powerful. Unfurling her power felt *right*. "So what do I have to do?"

"Nothing special really. You just keep working with me and your *maman*. I think having all of us work together would be a good thing. Your *maman* said you fed her power this afternoon?"

"Well, she was working a spell, I let some of my power flow to her."

"Did she tell you how?"

"No, I just touched her and sent it to her." She shrugged.

Tante Elise eyed her shrewdly. "Not very many witches can do that, you know, it's difficult to control. If you can do it so effortlessly, I think that we will be very powerful indeed." She stood and motioned around the apartment. "First things first. You must always sweep your apartment before you enter as I showed you earlier. It's basic security, you never know what is lying in wait for you, yes?"

Lee nodded. "Of course. I feel stupid for not thinking of it before."

Tante Elise let that go with a small smirk. "Let's get to work then, shall we?"

They spent the two hours warding her apartment and then walked over to the shop to redo the wards there. Lee took over at four to do her shift as well.

At closing time she locked up and stood out front with her sister and cousins. The older women were all upstairs watching *Jeopardy!*.

She and her cousins decided that they'd all go to dinner and dancing, the day was lovely and the night was sultry. It called for some serious fun.

Chapter Two

As Lee got dressed she couldn't keep her eyes off her new purchase hanging on the wall in her bedroom. Earlier in the day, she'd gone in to one of the shops on Royal where her paintings were on commission and had spent three hundred dollars because a painting had pulled at her. There was something incredibly compelling about it, it spoke to her, drew her in. She placed it in her bedroom, across from the bed so that she could look at it as she was going to sleep. It was very modern, an explosion of color and emotion, something she wouldn't normally have liked much less spent that kind of money on, but she knew she couldn't have left the shop without it.

After she'd changed into a flirty sundress and some sandals, she pulled her heavy hair back to the nape of her neck with a silver clip, careful to not catch the amulet that her mother had given her on her tenth birthday. She reached up to trace the stylized circle of three bent sevens wrought from silver that hung between her breasts. It was special. According to her mother, Annalisa Charvez, one of her foremothers had worn it. Of course now that she knew the whole story about the Compact and Annalisa's part in it, it felt even more special to her.

On the way out to her car, she pulled a sprig of jasmine off a bush and tucked it into her hair and breathed the night air into her lungs.

Walking around the corner to the garage, she had been watching the color of the night sky deepening and the stars beginning to wink, and in not paying attention, slammed into someone.

"I'm sorry, I was looking up at the sky," she said in apology and looked up into the face of her victim.

He smiled down at her and she blinked up at him several times. "The color, when it goes from dusky blue to the deeper blue of night," he said, his voice smooth and thick, like honey. It rolled over her skin and sang to her very DNA. Everything in her life seemed to click into place, the moment was meant to be, fated. She was face to face with her partner, her heart. She was unafraid, excited.

It was him, the man from her dreams. He was tall, with a mane of golden hair, his eyes were chocolate brown, or at least that's what they looked like by the light of the streetlamp. "I'm Aidan, Aidan Bell. I just moved here from Chicago."

She cleared her throat, willing her voice to come back. Heat coursed over her body and moisture pooled, the man did things to her. "Uh, Amelia Charvez, Lee. Your name sounds familiar." It tickled the back of her brain until she remembered the painting she'd bought earlier that day. "Oh wait, do you paint? I bought one of your paintings today."

He smiled and her heart thudded so hard against her chest she was afraid he'd be able to hear it. "Yes, that's me. Your work is at Lenora's gallery too, right? Beautiful. I'm honored you like my work." He *could* hear her heart pounding in her chest and felt satisfied that she was as affected by this meeting as he was.

"I love it. It's very bold, vivid." No wonder it had called to her, it was an extension of his soul.

He stared at her for a moment and she felt his power run along her skin. He was *more* than human, she could feel it. Tentatively, she sent her own power back at him and caressed him with it. He gasped and looked at her, eyes widened.

"This is going to sound weird, but can I take you to dinner tonight? I've only just moved to town and I don't know very many people," he said, unable to stop himself from reaching out to touch a tendril of her hair that had escaped the clip.

That little touch sent heat coursing through her body. When she found her voice she was proud that it didn't sound breathy. "Well, actually, I have plans to go to dinner and go dancing to some live music with some of my family. Would you like to join us?"

"Are you sure they won't mind? I haven't been much of anywhere but the French Quarter. I did a walking tour of the Garden District the other day but not much else."

"I'm sure. Jacques-Imo is here in the French Quarter but Maple Leaf is out a bit more, not too far. I can give you a guided tour of the Garden District if you like, I grew up there. Where do you live, by the way?"

He pointed to her building. "Here. I moved into number four a few days ago. I have been in Lafayette for the last two days though, dealing with some business matters."

She looked back to the large mansion that had been made into apartments. "You live right above me," she said with a smile. She was totally drawn to this man, she felt safe with him in a way she'd never felt with anyone before.

"Oh? Well, it's nice to have such beautiful neighbors. I've only met Mrs. Ellis and while she and her yappy dog are nice enough, you are certainly more pleasant to look at."

She laughed and hit the garage door opener. "Shall we, then?" She motioned to the car.

"Yes, let's." He squeezed himself into the car, navigating the narrow space between the door and the wall and she pulled back out.

She stopped four blocks away and picked up her sister, who cast an interested look at Aidan and got in the backseat.

"Emily Charvez, this is Aidan Bell, my new neighbor and a fellow painter. Aidan, this is my sister, Em."

Aidan smiled back at the willowy raven-haired woman. She watched him through big green eyes that sparked with intelligence and no small amount of curiosity. "Hi, Aidan," Em said with a sly smile and a discreetly raised eyebrow at her sister. "Everyone is going to meet us at the restaurant."

"Okay," Lee said and guided the car to Oak Street, and after a few minutes of concentrating by both women, a spot only a block away opened up and Lee pulled in with a satisfied smile.

"Wow, the parking gods must be with you. What a great spot," Aidan said with satisfaction as he got out of the car.

"Yeah, something like that." Lee winked at her sister. They walked up to the front of the restaurant and saw that the usual crowd was gathering. The place was so good that it always had a long waitlist for a table. Luckily, as it went with parking spots, so it went with restaurants and a table was waiting for them. They got seated and ordered drinks and the others began to show up, all with interested glances at Aidan.

Aidan was confused, curious and aroused. The woman beside him was the most alluring he'd ever met. He had no idea how to tell her he'd been dreaming of her for months or that he'd pulled up stakes in Chicago and headed south to New Orleans because his grandmother told him to pursue his dream woman. Half of him hadn't believed her, but there she was, and right underneath his nose.

He felt a total connection to her, like she was right for him, made for him. He felt a strong power in her, just barely beneath her skin, but he had no idea of how to broach the subject with her. He mentally snorted when he thought of it. *So, I'm a vampire, I've been having these dreams about you. I sense you and I are meant to be together. It seems like you are more than human, like me. What are you?*

The table was filled with Lee's siblings and cousins. Aidan looked at them as they interacted with each other. There was a lot of general good cheer between them all, a sort of ease that one only finds in a large family very rarely. They clearly loved and respected each other. He'd been surprised to meet Lee's brothers Eric and Niall. Unlike the dark-haired Em, they had sandy blond hair but the younger one had the same fey features that Lee had.

"So, Aidan, what brings you to New Orleans?" Lee's twin brother, Eric, asked, bringing Aidan out of his thoughts.

Lee rolled her eyes.

Aidan laughed. There had been several pointed, personal questions since they'd arrived. "I wanted a change, I've been feeling a need to move, to get out of a rut. My painting can be done anywhere really. My grandmother, she's the matriarch of my family, she suggested New Orleans. I visited and fell in love." He shrugged.

"So is your family ruled by women too?" Eric asked with a chuckle.

"Well, by my grandmother really. Why? Is yours?"

Lee's brothers laughed. "*That* is an understatement."

Lee looked into his chocolate eyes. "The women in our family are all very powerful. Not that the men aren't, it's just different. All are successful, intelligent people who are loved and respected by the women in my family."

"You said the women are powerful. Powerful how?"

She rolled her power over his skin like a cool caress, rolled it through him, wrapped it around him. His eyes widened and fluttered closed for a moment and then locked with hers, and she felt his power. Where hers was cool, his was warm, sultry where hers was crisp. Lee's power smelled clean, earthy, sharp like pine trees and a mountain stream. Aidan's was like honey, velvet, it rolled over her arms and legs, across her neck. She realized at last, what exactly his energy, his otherness was.

"I see," she said in a whisper.

He knew she was powerful but still didn't know exactly why. He did see that she knew what he was and made a mental note to speak with her about it when they were alone. He was relieved to see that she didn't seem frightened or repulsed by what he was, although from what he could feel, with power like hers there was very little in the world that she had to be frightened of.

Everyone was staring and then went back to their conversations and happy oohs and aahs when the food came. Afterwards, feeling full and satisfied, they all drove over to the Maple Leaf, where things were just getting started. They grabbed a patio table, it being already ridiculously hot and crowded inside.

"Shall we?" Aidan asked, pointing at the couples dancing on the sidewalk.

"Sounds good," she said and he took her off with a flourish and they joined the dancing couples under the stars.

As they danced, Aidan saw that her sister was deep in conversation with her brothers. They were obviously talking about him as they looked over to where he and Lee were dancing several times.

"Your family's staring," Aidan said into her ear.

Lee looked over his shoulder and smiled at him. "They're just trying to figure out if you're a threat to me."

"What do you think?"

"I think you're safe, even if you do need to take blood to live," she said.

"So you guessed huh? How much do you know about vampires?"

"I don't know very much. There are some here, of course. There's a bit of everything in New Orleans." She shrugged. "Shifters, vampires, ghosts, demons, witches, you name it, it's here."

"And what are you?"

"I'm a witch, a witch dreamer to be exact." He looked confused and she explained further. "A witch dreamer is a witch with a touch of clairvoyance. We have vivid dreams, often of future events or of people who are going to come into our lives. We can walk in dreams, go into other people's dreams and their subconscious. We can wield magic in dreams as well as in waking hours."

"Have you been walking in my dreams?"

"No. Generally, it's not something we do without permission, barring a threat. It's considered an offensive act, unnecessarily aggressive. Sometimes though, the dreams just happen and connect two people who are meant to be brought together for some reason. I have been dreaming of you for the last two months," she said, looking up at him.

They stared into each other's eyes for a long moment and she felt like he could see right down to her soul. She felt understood, not just in the sense of him being something more than simply human, but also like something inside of him recognized something inside of her. His hand was on her shoulder and his flesh against hers made her cells zing with life. She nearly felt giddy, being with him was so right, so good. Just having him touch her was deliriously wonderful. She'd never felt such a deep connection to anyone or anything in her life. This man was meant for her. The dreams were one thing, the reality was even better.

"I've been dreaming of you, too. I finally went to my grandmother over it, I was wondering if I was bespelled. She told me to come here."

"Oh, well, good," she said, a bit breathlessly.

"I can't believe I found you---that you are real." He touched her cheek with the back of his fingers and the electricity of the contact shot through her system.

"I'm glad you found me too, or that I found you. Whichever."

The rest of the evening passed in a haze for Lee, Aidan's very presence was soothing, relaxing. When everyone got up to go home Lee felt their regard for her and their curiosity about Aidan. Aidan stepped into the restroom and Em cornered her at the car.

"So? This is the dream man?" Em asked, her eyebrow raised.

Lee nodded. "Yeah. It's…" She shrugged, unable to put into words how much it all was, what it meant.

"He's no threat to you. He loves you, that came through so clearly. You know I can't read you but you both feel right together." Em looked her sister over and nodded as if making up her mind.

Lee grinned and hugged her sister. "Thanks! I know that I felt it on my own, but it's nice to know that you've given him the thumbs-up. Makes me feel safer."

"He's safe. Different. I can't tell just what, but he would die before he hurt you."

Lee was always impressed by her sister's ability to read people so well and she trusted that ability without question. Em was a woman of few words, shy, but intensely loyal and intelligent and one of the most empathic witches alive.

She dropped Em off at her apartment and they watched until she got safely inside and drove back to their building.

* * * * *

As they were walking around to the gates Lee felt it, the sickening shadow she'd felt earlier in the day.

She let down her shields and let her power unfurl around her. "Quickly, come with me," she said to Aidan and he followed her without a word. They went through the gates where Lee and *tante* Elise had laid a ward earlier that day. The shadow hesitated as it attempted to break through the warding. She pushed Aidan toward her door and tossed him the keys. He figured it was the one with the rubber doodad on it—with luck it was—and the door came open. He turned and saw her facing a dark shadow, her power crackling in the air around her. The hair on his arms rose.

Lee backed up toward the door and shoved him inside. He nearly ran back out again as he heard her shriek out in pain but she kept him back with her power and got inside herself, closing the door behind her. The psychic hit on the door was palpable but the shadow did not pass the wards on the door.

Lee felt the shadow probe the exterior walls, she felt its frustration, its rising anger. She'd been surprised at how powerful it was when it had whipped out, wounding her. Shoving that to the back of her mind, she took a deep breath and further loosed the reins on her power, standing there in the middle of the room, arms at her side, eyes closed, she sent her magic out like a bubble around herself, then Aidan, then the room, the apartment. She pushed it outside and exploded it against the shadow and it dispersed, unable to reform. She laid a spell of protection and slumped on the couch next to Aidan.

"What the fuck was that?" he asked, his voice deep and rumbly.

"Something dark, something evil, something powerful," she said and looked at him, his chocolate brown eyes were now more of an amber color. His voice had deepened.

"My bloodlust, it fights to the surface when I am threatened," he explained as his eyes bled back to their chocolate depths. "What happened?" He motioned to her shoulder, where she bore an angry-looking slash in her flesh.

"It felt like it whipped me with its power, it tore into my skin." She got up and went into the kitchen to press a clean, wet cloth on it. He took over for her and applied pressure. With his so the scent of her blood drove him crazy.

"You might want to purify this wound somehow. Do you have something here that might work?"

She smiled into his face. "My aunt makes a really excellent healing poultice. I'll pack the wound with that to drive out anything nasty. As the wound was caused by magic, it's helpful if I treat it with magic. In this case, my using the herbs that my aunt has put together should counteract the dark magic. She uses a healing spell when she makes the mixture. It's a great thing to have around the house."

"Ah, good idea. It doesn't smell infected or contaminated. Better to be safe though." He watched her as she worked, efficiently applying the sweet-smelling herb pack to the wound. "Did I feel it correctly, did it *know* you?"

"Yes, it knows me. It knows my power, it's attracted to me because of it. I'm all right, I'm glad to know the wards my great-aunt and I placed held it out. But it tasted me, my power and my blood." She didn't want to think of what that might mean.

"It stopped for a moment at the gate."

"Yes, as an afterthought earlier today, as we were leaving, we put a ward there. Just a light one, not like the ones here in the apartment. My *tante* Elise is so powerful that even an offhanded last-minute spell from her is strong enough to repel that shadow. Without the hesitation, well, I don't know that I'm strong enough to have held it off in the open just yet."

"Jesus."

"Not nearly close." She looked at him. "You ready to forget you ever met me and head back to Chicago?"

He took her hand and kissed her fingers. "No way. But, well, reinforcements might be in order. I know someone, one of my best friends, Alex. He's the son of one of the most powerful wizards in the country, and an accomplished wizard in his own right. He might be able to help. He may not be the same kind of practitioner you are, but he practices on the path of light."

"I've never met a wizard, but I hear they can be a bit snobby when it comes to dealing with witches. I've met male practitioners of black magic, but white magic is generally earth-based, nature-based. It's generally female. Your friend must be interesting indeed. But my mother is a witch, as is my great-aunt. I think I have the backup I need."

"Is your sister a witch too?"

"Technically yes, but not in the way I am. Em is a feeler, an empath if you like. She's got this great instinct about people, what their motivations are, if they are hiding something, but also about magic, too. Aside from that, she's an incredible researcher, her skills are amazing, I think it's part of her intuitiveness. She just knows stuff, it's impressive.

"The women, the Charvez women, are all born with some kind of talent. They can be healers, some like my grandmother and my aunt are able to read the future, or possible paths of the future, some are feelers. Only one Charvez woman a generation is a witch dreamer. My great-aunt, my mother and now me."

"Wow, pretty cool. We have talents, too. Each vampire has them, they are usually handed down from our makers. In my case, my parents because I was born a vampire but those who are bitten get them from their sire.

"My gift is in my voice, I have the ability to put humans in my thrall. I suppose it was handy back in the days when we used to take blood from them without their knowing about us. I can shapeshift as well, my animal is a wolf and I can be as insubstantial as mist."

She turned to him after checking the wound, which was already healing. "Really? I don't know anything about vampires at all."

"We can eat and drink and garlic isn't deadly to us. We don't need food like humans do to survive, that's what we need blood for. But I like a good plate of red beans and rice as much as the next guy."

She grinned at that. "Cool."

He laughed. "You aren't a bit afraid of me are you?"

"Do I think you're going to attack me?"

He nodded.

She shrugged. "I figure if I can fight off that nasty shadow, I can fight you off. Plus, I am sure my sister and cousin read you tonight and if you posed a threat to me, my family would have taken care of you. Lastly, my *tante* Lou read me, read my dreams, she told me you weren't a threat."

"I don't take blood from the unwilling, although I should tell you that blood and sex are very close together for vampires and I hope I'm not too forward by telling you that I hope to have sex with you soon. I would never hurt you, if you didn't want me to feed I wouldn't."

She nodded, thinking about it. "Do you have to stay out of the sun?"

"A newly changed vampire can be killed by the sun, but once you get to be about two hundred years old, you would just pass out and be powerless. The sun saps our energy. I work a lot during the early morning hours and at dusk, the light is perfect then."

"You said you were born a vampire? I never imagined that vampires had families."

"Yes, it's unusual but it happens. My parents live in Ireland, my grandmother in Chicago."

"Amazing. You learn something new every day." She smiled at him. She drank in the way he looked there in her apartment, in her life and she realized that with him in her life now, she had to protect him. He was vulnerable during part of the day, vulnerable to this thing that was stalking her.

"I want to ward your apartment. Would that be all right?"

"The shadow recognized me too," he said matter-of-factly.

"I think so. I just want you to be safe."

He smiled at her and leaned forward and kissed her gently, just the barest slide of his lips against hers. He backed up. "Shall we then? Do you need anything special to do this?"

"No, although I want you to wear something." She stood up and rustled through a wooden box on her bookcase. She pulled out an amulet on a silver chain. "It's an amulet of protection. It's enchanted." She handed it to him. The amulet was a long rectangle inlaid with Celtic symbols. "It's Celtic magic, appropriate for an Irishman." She smiled and he put it on. It was warm against his chest.

He held out his hand and pulled her to him. "Thank you," he whispered and leaned down to capture her lips with his own. His power met hers and they melded. Her lips were soft but firm, her bottom lip was so juicy he wanted to bite it, but he held back. He traced their outline with his tongue and she opened beneath him and his tongue flowed into her mouth like honey. Her taste hit his system like a jolt of electricity straight to his cock, setting his brain on fire. His need for her began to hum in his ears like the rushing of the wind.

She wanted to groan when she felt his body tighten against hers. She wanted to rub herself all over him, to slide herself across him like a cat. His energy, warm and sensual, ran through her and she felt her own cool energy sinuous against it, felt his breath hitch at the sensuality of it. Her hands wove through his silken hair while his slowly ran up and down her back. She molded her body against his, glorying in the way they felt together.

He pulled back, his eyes glittering, a smile on his face. "You taste so good, like cinnamon and vanilla," he said, his voice making her nipples hard, sending waves of molten heat to her pussy.

"Your voice," she said, breathless, rubbing her nipples across his chest and reveling in the sensation.

His grin promised wicked things. Naughty naked things. "It's not intentional, you bring it out in me."

"I like it, do it again."

He laughed and set her away from him. His incisors were lengthening already, he had shaky control at best. He wanted her to be one hundred percent aware and willing when they made love---before and if, they shared blood. At the moment, they were both a bit off balance, the power of their union had left them both a bit shaky.

"Come on, let me show you my lair," he said in a goofy, fake Transylvanian accent.

He opened the door and she followed him up the wrought iron stairs to his door. He unlocked it and stood aside to let her in first.

She looked around. His personal style was a lot like his paintings—the colors bold, the furniture modern. He'd used it in the same way she had, his studio using the same eastern-facing space, meaning his bed was directly above hers. "My apartment is set up this way too. You'll be sleeping above me."

"Oh, I hope so," he said and she laughed.

"That too, but you know what I mean."

He nodded. "Do you need me to do anything special while you lay the wards?"

"No. But, Aidan, are you helpless when you are sleeping?"

"Well, not totally, but the zenith of the day is when I'm weakest. I can be awakened but it's very hard for me to be up and around. It takes an extraordinary event—a lot of adrenaline—to make it happen."

"Okay. The reason I ask is because I want to place the strongest wards in the place where you are weakest. So let me do your bedroom first. You can be out here or in there, it won't affect me," she said absently.

He lay across his bed and watched as she drew sigils in the air and softly spoke the words of the spell. He felt the air knit together as she marked the space. She moved out of the room, providing extra warding at the ceiling, windows, door and walls of his room and then worked her way through the rest of the apartment.

After nearly two hours she sat down on his couch, exhausted. He sat next to her and pulled her into his arms. "Thank you," he said against her hair. He felt a sense of comfort with her that he'd only had with his family. He felt utterly safe with her, like he'd known her forever. He knew that he loved her and that she loved him as well. It was disconcerting and yet it felt utterly natural.

"You're welcome. Tell me about yourself," she said against the skin of his throat. His pulse jumped as her lips moved over the jugular vein.

"Are you all right? You seem tired." He pulled the bandage back and examined the wound. "It looks good, it's almost gone. That must be some kind of supercharged herbal concoction."

"My cousin is a gifted healer. It should be gone by morning. I don't feel anything wrong at this point. I just need to take care of myself tonight."

"What can I do to help?" he asked.

"I'm tired, I've worked a lot of magic today, more than I ever have before. I'll be fine, I have some herbs at my place. If I burn them as I sleep they aid me in recovery."

"Then let's get you back to your place and get that started." He stood and picked her up, cradling her against his chest.

"Hey, I can walk!"

"I know, I like holding you like this. It's not a chore."

"I'm heavy."

He snorted in disbelief. "Even if I were a mortal man you wouldn't be heavy, but I'm not mortal, I have quite of bit of strength, I can handle a little bit of a woman like you."

He walked out, locking the door behind him and they took the stairs back to her apartment. He took her inside and set her down.

"Are you trying to ditch me?" she asked him with a grin as she pulled out the bag of healing herbs she'd picked up at the shop earlier that week. The special mixture was one that she always kept around, it helped to relax her, to purify her spirit and the air. She filled the teakettle with water, put it on the flame and placed a cheesecloth bag filled with the herbs in a teapot and then took the rest and placed them in a special burner and lit it, saying a brief spell for healing and cleansing. Within moments a sweet, refreshing smell was in the air.

"Ditch you? Because I didn't ravish you on my couch? Not at all. You don't know how much I want you, how much I want to be with you. I just want you to take care of yourself."

She turned to him and walked into his arms. Looking up into his face she said seriously, "I do know, I feel it too. It feels so natural to be with you, like I've known you forever. I'm not one to be silly over men, I date very rarely and I've never felt very deeply about anyone other than the members of my family. I bumped into you seven hours ago and suddenly I feel so…" she sighed, searching for what it is she felt.

Aidan put his finger to her lips. "You feel love. That I make you whole. I make you feel fulfilled in a way you've never imagined you could. You didn't realize how empty you had felt until you looked into my eyes and that emptiness was gone," he said softly.

She nodded.

"I know. Because I feel it too." His eyes seemed to see right to her heart, to her soul.

The kettle began to hum and she poured the water into the teapot to steep. "Can I get you anything? You look a bit pale yourself."

"I haven't fed. I need to."

She thought for a moment and went to him, kneeling between his thighs. "I can help. Take my blood. At this point, I've done enough checking to be sure it hasn't been tainted."

His eyes bled to the amber color they'd been earlier. He could smell the sweetness of her blood, he knew that she wasn't infected by the darkness. He swallowed, pushing his intense desire for her down, needing to put her first. "No, you're tired from working. If I took your blood it would only make you more tired. I have some donors here in town, people who willingly give me blood. I'll go to one of them when I've seen you to bed."

She turned away and stood up, bustling around the kitchen. He could feel her broadcasting jealousy as she worked. He felt her confusion and resentment. He'd never been able to sense emotions like that before. He went to her.

"Lee, what is it?"

"It's stupid."

He tipped her chin so that he could see her face. "No it isn't. Talk to me."

"Well, you said sex and blood were very close for vampires."

He nodded, still not understanding why she was so upset.

She gave an exasperated sigh. "I know I don't have any claims on you but I don't like the idea of you having a sexual anything with anyone but me." She crossed her arms, looking miserable.

He laughed and the velvety sound caressed her skin, causing her nipples to tighten and warmth to radiate through her body.

She widened her eyes at him, her lips parted. He leaned in and kissed her softly.

"Lee, darlin', yes, it's true that it's a bit sexual when I feed but it's just part of the process. For the donor, it's an incredible sexual rush, an extraordinary climax. It's why the donors like to donate. For me, it's more like a rush of euphoria. If I'm sexually attracted to the donor it usually does move into sex but it won't be like that tonight or ever again. It's nothing like how it will be between you and me when we make love because you're my mate and they're donors. There is more than just blood between us, there's heart, soul, connection."

"That's supposed to comfort me?" She hated feeling such turmoil. She'd never felt this sort of jealousy. "Look, never mind, you have to have it to live and I'd rather have you alive and sort of having sex with someone else than not alive."

"But it's not sex, not really." He had rarely taken human women as partners for a reason. He found them very hard to understand. A female vampire knew what it meant to feed.

She rolled her eyes. "Only a man could say something so dumb. People climax, you said. One person making another person climax, that's sex." She sighed. "Look, how would you like it if I got another man off? If simply by my doing something to him he had an outrageous orgasm, and I got off on it too?"

He frowned, not liking the thought of her getting anyone off but him. "It's merely a side effect of the feeding."

She drank her tea and the color began to return to her face. He watched her, satisfied that she'd recover. The sweet herbs in the air made him feel cleansed and calm.

"I can just not feed tonight. It won't be a big deal," he said, hating that she was feeling jealous.

"Don't be silly, Aidan. You're pale, you need it. I'll get over it, I'm a big girl. I just don't want to hear about it or know who any of your donors are." *The sluts*, she thought darkly.

"I hate that you feel bad. I don't want any other woman. For me, from the moment I saw you it's been you and you only. The climax is a result of giving blood, aside from that, it means nothing to me. I do appreciate my donors, of course, they do me a great honor by sharing their blood with me, but you are *mine*. You complete me in a way that, in the two hundred and forty-five years I've been alive, I never thought possible. Please don't feel that I'm cheating." He pushed a curl back behind her ear.

She nodded, her eyes were still sad. "I don't, truly. It's just going to take some getting used to. I should go to bed now. I have to work with my mother and great-aunt tomorrow and I need to be rested."

He pulled her into his arms. "Let me help you. Let's get you into the shower and into some pajamas. Once I've tucked you in I'll go."

She quirked a small grin at that. "You're going to help me get in the shower?"

"Well, I'll stand guard outside the door to be sure you don't fall or anything. I don't know whether I could stand to walk out your door tonight if I saw you naked."

"How much blood do you need?" she asked, a sensuous thickness in her voice.

He shook his head vehemently. "No. I need more than you can give and I want our first time to be free from worry."

She gave a pretty pout and he took her bottom lip between his teeth. One of his incisors nicked the fullness there and her blood touched his tongue. Her taste exploded into his system. She was rich and deep and velvet, she was power and light and goodness, she was sex and love and siren and angel. He moaned deep in his throat, his tongue sweeping over the cut, drawing more of her essence into his body.

She clutched at him, her hands in his hair, her tongue running over the sharp edges of his extended incisors, inciting him further. She was so wet, so soft and slick with wanting him that she was sure her panties were drenched. She ground herself against him, aching to make contact, needing him desperately.

He could feel how much she wanted him and it was driving him wild. She was so alive under his hands, so soft and beautiful, so sexy. He wanted nothing more than to sink his teeth and his cock deep within her right that moment. But she had expended so much energy that he was worried about her. With all of his willpower he stepped back, holding her away from his body.

"You taste like the finest wine, the sweetest chocolate, the earthiest ale. You intoxicate me, Lee." His voice seduced her without his even meaning to. "I have to go now, before I take you here against the wall, despite your weakness." He kissed a finger and pressed it to her lips. "I'll call you in the late afternoon tomorrow, when I get up," he said softly and was gone before she'd even blinked.

* * * * *

Aidan called his grandmother in Chicago when he got home from feeding.

"I've found her, Nan. She's a witch. God, Nan, she's so beautiful, small, almost fey and powerful. So powerful you can feel it just standing near her. I have never felt this way about any woman. You won't believe this, but she lives right below me."

His grandmother chuckled. "It just means I was right, you and she are meant for each other. And of course she's powerful, you need a powerful woman at your side. Didn't I tell you to listen to those dreams?"

"Thanks, Nan, you were right and I'm so glad. I'm just sorry I'll only have a human lifetime with her."

But all she would say was, "Don't be so sure. I've got to go, love, the sun has risen and I need to call my broker. I love you. I'll make plans to come down your way to meet this girl, shall I?"

"I love you too, Nan, and yes, I'd love for you to meet her. She's incredible." He hung up, going into his studio to work. He could feel Lee's essence in his apartment, the wards she'd placed were like protective arms around him.

Chapter Three

Lee woke up refreshed and relaxed. She made coffee in the French press and ate a baguette with the plum preserves that Georgie had given her the day before. She sat near the open window and did her daily meditation and centering exercises. She felt different that morning, as if the day before she'd been a small stream but now she was the ocean. Her powers had truly begun to course through her body and she embraced the enormity of them.

The day was already warming up and she threw on a sundress and some sandals, pulled her hair back, put on the pair of silver hoops her brother had given her for her last birthday and she was off. A look up toward Aidan's place showed her that his curtains were drawn tightly against the daylight. She reached out toward him and found his essence at rest. She mentally checked the wards, and relieved, noted that they were all still standing and hadn't been tested.

Across the street from the shop she looked up and saw Vivienne Porter. She stood tall against the bright blue sky, her skin was the color of dark chocolate, her hair wrapped in a multicolored head wrap. She was imposing and regal and her power radiated from her. Vivienne was a local voodoo priestess and a good friend of the Charvez family. "Lee, a word if you please?" she called out with a wave.

Lee walked across the street and kissed the other woman's cheeks. "How you be?" she asked with a smile.

"I'm troubled, Lee. Last night we were in the middle of a rite, nothing complex or anything but a dark presence manifested. Right there in the living room. It was bad and we all had to work together to push it out. I haven't seen anything this bad in decades. It felt…"

"Like oil? Dark and sticky and toxic?" Lee said quietly.

"Ah, you felt it too? Yes, exactly like that. Even left a film of nastiness behind it. Don't know what it wanted, felt like it wanted in, wanted us. We might all have to work together on this thing before too long. I wanted to warn you and your family, I expect we might be in for a fight sometime."

"I'll tell *grandmere* and *tante* Elise. We felt it yesterday. Vivienne, you did ward your place, right? This thing, it comes back, it *recognizes*."

They both shuddered. "Yes, of course, I advised all of my people to do the same. We are going to stick to only one or two places for rites and ceremonies for the time being, those places we can protect better."

"Good idea. Keep us updated and we'll do the same. *Namaste*, Viv," Lee said, touching her forehead and her heart.

"God Bless," Vivienne replied and they both went their separate ways.

Lee walked into the shop and the smell of the herbs that were burning hit her. She had to hold onto the doorjamb as a waking dream hit her.

A dark-haired man approached her, holding out his hand. He was powerful, like her. Eyes as green as the leaves on a magnolia tree. He was smiling but wary, the way he was standing screamed out that he was protecting her. When she took his hand something shifted in her soul, all of the pieces fit and she was shining bright. Aidan was there and was smiling at her and the dark man. *Triad*.

She came back to herself, blinking. Em and her mother were standing in front of her, looking interested. Her *grandmere* pushed between them and took Lee's hand, brushing cool fingertips across her forehead. "Triad. Three. Very powerful. He comes, Lee, and soon. You will need him."

Her *grandmere* kissed her cheek and handed her a glass of lemonade and walked back to the counter where her mother, *tante* Elise and sister were standing, waiting somewhat impatiently for an explanation. Her *grandmere* frequently did things of that nature, she'd walk up to you, touch you and say or do something that made you feel as if she'd looked inside your head.

Lee told them about the dream, about Aidan and what he was, about the attack on her at her apartment and about what Vivienne had told her.

"Busy day already, sug," Em said.

"What is this Aidan like?" her mother asked suspiciously.

"He loves her, *maman*. He feels fulfilled by her, he sees her and her only. He means no harm," Em explained.

"I can't explain it but I love him too. I'm not impulsive, you know me, and yet, I just wanted to jump into bed with him last night. He could have, I wanted it, but I'd just warded his apartment and he was worried that I was too tired and weak."

"Did he take your blood?" *Tante* Elise asked.

"The shadow, it injured me." Lee showed them the spot that had healed to all but a red mark overnight. "It was bleeding, looked like a whip slash. Anyway, he looked mighty interested when I was cleaning it up but his first thought was to be sure the wound wasn't tainted. Since I couldn't be sure right then, I held back. Later, after I'd used the healing herbs, I could feel that my blood was fine and he nicked my lip when we kissed but he wouldn't take any more. I offered, more than once even, but he wouldn't, said he didn't want to do anything to hurt me. I feel with all of my heart, with all of my talent, that he would never hurt me."

"And you don't think a vampire taking your blood is harm?" her mother said calmly.

"I've thought of that but I keep coming back to my base feelings from the dreams and from being with Aidan. I feel that blood exchange between us is important somehow. That far from harming me, it'll help."

"I see that too," *grandmere* said from the counter. "And if Em feels it—" she shrugged, "—we know we can trust it."

Tante Elise, Lee and her mother went into the largest room in the back, a place frequently used by the Charvez women to rest or take some time out from a shift. Sitting for a few minutes, they discussed the information Vivienne had brought them before they got down to working on magic. The back of the shop was closed off from the retail space so they could work without being interrupted.

After they'd sorted through what they knew, they decided to continue on as they were, with Lee practicing each day with *tante* Elise and her mother. "Three is important in many ways. A triad of witches creates a circuit of power," *tante* Elise said and Lee nodded. "But I think there's more than just the three of us to your being the key here in defeating this dark power."

Lee nodded, she thought so too but she couldn't quite put her finger on exactly what it was that made her feel that way.

Accepting that there were things that they didn't know but still had to move forward, *tante* Elise made a nod with her head as if moving on. "Today I want you to work on sending your power out as an offensive weapon. Let's try bolts of flame and electricity." *Tante* Elise stood and she and Lee's mother showed Lee how to reach into her power and transform it into a physical weapon.

Aside from being a sort of breakroom, the space was also primed for working magic. It was warded against magical intrusion from the outside, the walls had protective runes painted on them and the flooring was charmed in a way that allowed them to pull their power from the earth below.

It took a while for Lee to get the hang of it, to be able to reach in and pull out something tangible. Elements, while being a part of her natural ability to control, were still tricky to contain and wield, especially inside. She envisioned the flame as a physical thing and learned to contain it to keep from hurting herself. She felt odd holding a ball of flame in her hand. It didn't burn her but when she hurled it at a covered target, it scorched the flameproof material. She was beginning to feel that she could actually defeat this new bad boy in town.

Lee headed home, anxious to see Aidan again. She quickly changed her clothes and was opening her door to go and see him just as he began to knock.

"Hi, you look much better today," he said with a smile.

"Come in," she invited and he did, looking sinfully handsome in a pair of white linen pants and a wine-colored shirt with a banded collar, not a bead of sweat in sight.

Lee shut the door and he pulled her to him, capturing her lips under his own. "I missed you," he said against her lips.

"Me too," she said, smiling.

"You feeling better?" He peeked at her shoulder, and saw the creamy skin that was now unmarked. He gave her a satisfied look with a bit of promise at the edges.

"Much," she answered, running her hands up his chest, needing to feel him, to touch him.

"I love it when you touch me," he said. He pulled her in closer, his hands cradling the flesh of her ass, kneading it in his long-fingered hands. The fingertips just grazed her pussy lips. "I want you so much I'm dizzy with it," he said as he nibbled on her ear.

"Me too," she replied, unbuttoning his shirt and kissing the bare flesh that was revealed. She pulled the tail of his shirt out of his trousers, ran her hands along the skin of his back and pushed the shirt off. "You're beautiful," she said softly.

He was tall and lean and muscled like a cyclist or a runner. He had a smattering of honey-colored hair over his chest. She grinned as she took in the trail of hair that started at his navel and disappeared below the waistband of his pants. She had plans for that later that included her tongue. His skin was like velvet and she stroked him with her hands, feeling as if she'd die if she couldn't crawl into him, touch every inch of him.

"No, *you're* beautiful," he said and popped the buttons of her bodice. The dress slid off her shoulders, revealing the creamy curves of her unclad breasts capped by pretty coral-colored nipples that were hard and begging for his attention. "No bra." He smiled down at her. She looked down as his hands cupped her breasts and his thumbs flicked over the nipples.

"It's so hot and they aren't that big anyway," she said, breathless.

"They're perfect. I love the way they fill my hands." He was doing that magic with his voice again, the sound of it brushing over her, sending liquid desire to her sex, making her knees turn to jelly.

"I like the way they fill your hands too," she said faintly as he lowered his mouth, first kissing the upper curve of each breast and then — she thought she might faint when his mouth covered her nipple — swirling his tongue around the hardened peak. "Oh yes," she breathed out as each tug of his mouth, each graze of his teeth, each insistent flick of his tongue shot straight to her pussy.

He pulled back, looking into her face. Her gaze was blurred by desire, pupils wide. Her lips were slightly parted and swollen from his kisses. She tasted like the best thing he'd ever imagined. Her skin under his fingers, his tongue, drove him insane. Her smell, a combination of heady flowers and crisp air, was rising from her skin as she heated with passion. He breathed her in and his cock twitched in response.

She had a smattering of freckles across her collarbone and he leaned down and laved them with the flat of his tongue, tasting her, pulling her into him as he did. She shivered and made such a sexy sound that he had to close his eyes and count to ten. He was perilously close to tossing her on the bed and plunging inside of her, both with his cock and his teeth. In all of the years he'd been alive, never had he felt so out of control.

Lee could feel the tension just under the surface that he was holding himself in check and it made her crazy to know that *she* made him feel that way. Smiling softly, promises in her eyes, she took his hand and led him into her bedroom.

She'd known they would end up either in her bed or his and so she'd prepared. She'd spoken a cleansing spell after she'd changed her clothes earlier, the room felt safe, intimate, almost like a cocoon, a space that was untouched by the uncertainty of the world outside because it was just the two of them and they were protected. She had also covered her windows with heavy-backed curtains in a deep eggplant color in case he ever slept over. Her bed was waiting with fresh sheets, washed with a bit of lavender thrown in. When she shut the door behind them, it felt as if the world had been left behind and that nothing and no one else existed but the two of them.

Aidan watched her walk. She wore nothing more than a whisper-thin pair of pink panties. He reached up and pulled the clip from her hair, releasing her curls with his fingers, stroking them over her scalp. Her eyes slowly closed and she moaned at the feeling.

Her hands slid down the wall of his chest, her fingertips making a tour of his belly button. She traced the trail of hair leading south, below the waist of his pants, then looked up into his eyes and gave him such a wicked look that he nearly began to pant. The angel had turned siren and his body and spirit were all for it.

Lee sat on the edge of her bed and pulled him so that he was standing in front of her. She leaned in and ran her cheek across his flat, firm abdomen, breathing him in. The smell of hot, hard and aroused male hit her senses along with that chemical mix of pheromones that was uniquely Aidan. She laid a series of openmouthed kisses across his abdomen. Running her fingertips through the line of hair heading to his groin she looked up at him, opening herself so that he could see just how much she wanted him. "I love this trail. I need to see where it ends up," she said, voice smoky. She slowly unbuttoned and unzipped his pants and pushed them and his silk boxers down his hips. He stepped out of them, kicking them aside with his shoes.

His cock jutted up proudly, so hard it nestled against his stomach. She smiled at him, rubbed her cheek along his silky skin and purred at the heat of it and the way he felt against her. She flicked out the tip of her tongue and lapped up the bead that had pearled on the tip, pausing to dip into the slit and eliciting a gasp of pleasure from him.

Teasing him, she breathed over the head of his cock and moved upwards, taking small, sharp nips at his lower belly and his navel, then laving the sting. His hands were clenching and unclenching at his sides. She tipped her head back and locked eyes with him and felt the depth of their connection deep in her soul.

Aidan ran his hands through the auburn curls around her face, cradling her head gently. She broke his gaze and trailed her tongue down that trail of fine blond hair that fascinated her so and down the length of his cock and to his balls. He trembled when she took each sensitive globe into her mouth, sucking it gently. "Oh god," he mumbled, his hands tightening in her hair.

Smiling, she moved up, stopping to lightly suck and nibble the spot just under the cock head. She slowly sank her mouth onto his cock, tongue swirling over the purpled crown. He gasped around his lengthening incisors, pulled into the sensation of her hot wet mouth sliding over him, the trust of having another person hold him in her mouth. "Oh yes, Lee, that's it. You feel so good," he broke out.

He was almost more than she could take into her mouth, she breathed slowly and let herself get accustomed to his size, to the taste and feel of him. She breathed his scent into her body and each time he let out a groan or gasp it tightened the coil of need low in her gut. Her nipples were diamond-hard, her breasts heavy, her pussy weeping. She imagined that instead of stroking her mouth over him she was riding him, his cock buried deep inside of her.

The rhythm she set was almost dreamy, he was entranced by her, by the way she was making him feel. The heat of her mouth as she engulfed him, the wetness of her saliva, the smooth flicks and swirls of her tongue pushed him higher. She raked her nails lightly over his balls and he groaned. He was getting close and as much as he craved coming in her mouth, filling her throat with his seed, he wanted to be deep inside her pussy when he came. "Lee, baby, stop. I want to be inside of you when I come," he said, his voice wrapping around her like a caress.

She pulled back reluctantly and gave a last, reverent kiss to the head of his cock. He pulled her to standing and got rid of her pretty pink panties. Standing back, he took in the sight of her. She was small, curvy, her breasts capped with those lovely coral nipples. He followed the line of her body, the small span of her waist, the flare of her hips and thighs, for a small woman her legs were long and strong. The small feet with the pink nails did him in. Her hair fell down about her shoulders, an errant curl swirled around one of her nipples. She made him breathless, blind with wanting.

He laid her back on the bed and kissed across her collarbone, laving the hollow of her throat. He kissed the curves of her breasts, burying his face in the valley between them, licking up the sides, paying extra attention to her nipples. He slowly sucked one nipple into his mouth and then quickly flicked his tongue over it again and again. When he bit the nipple and sucked hard, pulling it to the roof of his mouth, her back bowed and her hips arched into him. He could feel how juicy she was as her pussy rubbed along his abdomen. Her nails began to curl into the flesh of his shoulders and he reveled in the moans and squeals of pleasure she was making.

Reluctantly, he moved his mouth away from her breasts and kissed a line down her belly, running fingertips over each rib. He nibbled on her navel and kissed through her curls and down her leg, laving the vein on her inner thigh where he could feel her pulse strongly.

He pushed her thighs apart, sliding the palms of his hands upward, dipping his thumbs between her labia, spreading her wetness over her, feeling how soft and swollen she was for him. He parted her and looked down at her sex, glistening with want. "Such a gorgeous pussy. I can't wait to taste you," he said, using the full power of his voice to push her higher, to wrap her body with want and need. Lee moaned when it hit her body—his voice felt like another set of hands caressing her. She arched her hips up, trying to make contact with any part of him.

Just before she opened her mouth to beg, he lowered his mouth to her and bestowed a kiss so devastating that she was unable to stop from rolling her hips up, pressing her sex into his face and her power arced off his. The room was heavy with magic and power, with desire and sex. His tongue swept a circular arc from her gate, that sweet entrance of her pussy, then upwards to her clit. He put her thighs up onto his shoulders to get better access to her flesh. Opened up so fully to him, he ravaged every inch of her, spearing her with his tongue, delivering a gentle fucking. He was drowning in her, pressing his face into her pussy and moving from side to side. Her thighs trembled against his shoulders, but he was relentless.

She was creamy and salty-sweet, her taste like a drug to his system. He lapped at her swollen flesh, drinking her in. He eased a finger inside of her and his cock twitched as he felt how tight she was and how scalding hot. He needed to taste her pleasure. He hungered to hear her cry out as her climax hit. He slid another finger inside of her and latched onto her clit, sucking it hard into his mouth, feeling it bloom and harden against his tongue. He flicked his tongue up underneath it, using a quick and hard rhythm, pushing her relentlessly toward release, fingers stroking into her juicy flesh, incisors out and ready to sink into her.

Lee had never felt so utterly submerged in pleasure before. Her limbs felt heavy with it, her muscles burned and twitched as the incredible sensations surged through her. Her hands were sifting through his silky hair, pulling him against her. She could feel that her orgasm was quickly taking over her body. Her toes began to curl and she could swear her teeth were tingling.

Aidan felt her climax approach, could feel her body tighten and ready for the moment to come and when it did, when she cried out his name and her back bowed off the bed, hands fisting in his hair, he felt it all the way to his soul as she wrapped herself around his heart and settled there.

He continued to gently lap at her pussy, taking her sweet cream into his mouth, tasting her on his tongue until all of the orgasm had ridden through her body.

"I need to be inside of you," he said and she nodded eagerly. "I don't need a condom, we don't carry human STDs and we cannot make offspring with humans."

"Yes, yes, just fuck me. Oh god, please, Aidan, get inside of me," she begged and he moved up, accommodating himself between her thighs. He couldn't resist running the head of his cock through her wet pussy folds, coating himself with her honey, before he centered himself and thrust inside of her, seating himself in one hard movement, both of them sighing.

She felt so tight and hot that he wasn't sure he could move. She put her legs around his waist, opening herself to him fully. Cradling his jaw with her hands she looked into his eyes. "You and I, we are one, one heart, one soul. My life force is yours for pleasure and for sustenance."

He blinked at her recitation of the ritual words. "Where did you hear that?" he whispered around his incisors.

"I don't know. It just seemed the right thing to say. Did I say something wrong? I just wanted you to know that you could take blood from me because I love you."

He smiled. "No, you said it perfectly. It's a…sort of ritual of binding of two vampires. Like a marriage."

"Oh." She blushed.

"No, don't be embarrassed. I love you and I am humbled by your offering. It will be very pleasurable. I'm told that between mates the blood exchange is incredible. If you would like, the ritual is sealed by you taking in my blood. It won't hurt you, in fact, it should help you, make you stronger."

"Sealed how?"

"Blood is the essence of life, there is a lot of power in the exchange or spilling of it. Taken with the words, in essence, a spell is created that binds two like souls. When we've bound ourselves together, it's as if you inherited my strength too, and I yours. Not that we get the other's powers specifically, but that we'll be wrapped into one unit in many ways."

During this she'd been wriggling beneath him and distracting him. He kissed her neck and pulled nearly all of the way out and slid back in, causing a little distraction of his own. Seeing her eyes go a bit blurry and hearing her strangled moan, he added with a chuckle, "I already know you are my mate, we're meant to be together so I don't need any formal declaration. The dual exchange is part of the binding ceremony. Afterwards, we'd be seen as a bonded couple, a married couple, if you will, in the eyes of my culture. My protection would extend to you and yours and my family would protect you too."

"And you'd like that?"

"Very much. But I don't want to rush you," he added. The prospect of binding in a ceremony as old as his culture, of achieving what so many of his people looked lifetimes for thrilled through his system. Possessiveness sang like a drug through his veins.

She squeezed her inner muscles around him and arched her hips. "Let's do it," she said, looking into his eyes, nothing but yearning and love in them.

"I love you, Lee." He took a deep breath and began to thrust in and out of her. Her flesh sucked at him each time he began to pull away, as if she couldn't bear to let him leave her body. She felt so right, immediately their rhythm was perfect and she arched her head back. He repeated the words back to her and ran his sharp incisors over the vein-rich skin just above her left breast. Her blood flowed and he latched on, drinking her essence, feeling unnamable ecstasy as he swallowed her life force over and over.

The feel of him taking her blood, of his lips on the flesh of her breast, his tongue urging the thick velvet fluid into his mouth, the sound of him taking her into his body was too much. She felt like she'd stuck her finger into an electrical outlet but instead of pain, she was receiving a shock of pleasure so intense she'd never imagined it could be so good. Her climax hit, her pussy spasming around his cock, gushing cream, her toes curling. Her nails raked up his back and she cradled his head to her.

He laved his tongue along the incision to close it and had to shut his eyes as her blood charged him. Just those few moments of feeding from her were like he'd drank from four people. He was energized and just a bit intoxicated by her power.

Her eyes opened lazily and she looked up at him with a sexy smile. "Lee, you taste so good. Like nothing I've ever tasted before but something I have craved all of my life." He panted as he slid in and out of her. Running his sharp incisors over his wrist, he moved so that he could hold it to her mouth. "Drink from me, beloved."

She was hesitant but pushed past it and grabbed his wrist and held it to her lips, pulling his blood into her mouth. She was prepared to be disgusted but wasn't at all. He tasted so good, so right. She swallowed over and over, taking him into her. He stiffened and hoarsely shouted her name as he climaxed. She could taste his desire, his fulfillment, his love, on her tongue.

He pulled his wrist back and ran his tongue along the incision and it began to heal immediately. "That was…I don't have the words. I've never experienced that before," he panted out as he collapsed beside her, a long leg over her thighs.

"Experienced what? This is all new and incredible to me." She tried to concentrate on what he was saying but ripples of pleasure still rolled through her body, distracting her.

"I've had blood exchanges during sex with other vampires but I've never climaxed like that. You feel so amazing. When your mouth was on me, I thought I was going to pass out." He smiled at her and caught something not-so-happy in her eyes.

"What? Did it disgust you?" he asked softly.

"No," she said in a huff. "It was wonderful."

"Lee, you're pouting, why?"

"Why do you have to bring up sex with other women when you are still sweating from coming with me?"

"I was trying to tell you how wonderful it was. I thought a comparison would be helpful."

"Helpful? Aidan, I don't know what vampire women are like but human women, at least this one, don't like to hear about the other people their partners have been with—particularly during, or just after, they've had sex. I know you aren't a virgin, you're two hundred and forty-five years old, for goodness sake! Hell, you might even have had wives before me, but I really don't want to think about you being with anyone else. I know it's silly to be jealous, but I am."

His annoyance melted away and he tipped her chin so that she was looking at him. "Baby, I apologize most sincerely for hurting you. We're married now, you know, and in my culture that's a big deal. No, I've never been married before. I haven't even really been in love before. You are it, the first and only. There is no one else for me." He kissed her nose.

"Aidan, so, uh, the climax I had when you fed, is that what your donors feel?"

"I doubt it could be that beautiful or that intense but something like that."

"I don't want you feeding on anyone but me from now on," she said and he chuckled, pulling her closer to his body. "Don't laugh, I mean it. I had no idea I was a jealous person until yesterday, but apparently I am."

"Well, my love, judging from the way just a few swallows of your blood has made me feel, that won't be a problem. Your blood seems to have immense power in it, as you yourself do. I fear that you've spoiled me for anyone else's blood forever."

"Well, good. Your blood, and please don't be offended but I was worried it would be gross, but your blood was sweet and a bit tangy. Very nice," Lee said with a smile.

He threw back his head and laughed. "Why, thank you. Now, since I've hurt your feelings, let me make it up to you." He picked her up and put her astride his body. "Ride me, Lee. I want to look up and see your face above me," he whispered and she rose up, rubbing her soft pussy flesh over him and then sinking down on his cock, shudders of electric pleasure shooting down her spine as her wet flesh surrounded his. "Oh, that's the ticket, love."

He loved fucking her that way, her breasts gently swaying above him. He watched the curve of her flesh, ending at the coral-pink nipple. Her fat, glorious nipples that were so sensitive, so beautiful. Her stomach, softly curved, that small patch of mahogany curls at the apex of her thighs. He loved the way her thigh muscles bunched and relaxed as she moved on him. Her eyes took on a slumberous look, glazed over as if she were stoned with lust, lashes at half-mast. Her lips full and wet, swollen from their kisses, slightly parted, her hair curling forward.

She arched her back and he slid in deeper and she moaned low. He wished he could freeze this exact moment in time. He caressed her stomach and palmed her nipples, sliding one hand down to flick his thumb over her clit. "Yes," she raggedly whispered. Her skin glistened with sweat and her hair slid forward over her breasts like a silken curtain. As she moved he caught tantalizing glimpses of those pretty coral nipples through it.

"Come for me, Lee. Give it to me. Milk my cock," he whispered and he felt her tighten around him. Her hands slid back, reaching to caress his balls, rolling them gently. Her pussy was gripping his shaft, milking him with the motion of her orgasm. She was panting and silently screaming. He followed her then, loosing himself inside of her in pulse after heated pulse as she rose up and slammed down on him over and over, her head whipped back, breasts arched forward. Her orgasm rocked her, she trembled and vibrated with it. She felt complete, unraveled and reknit. With a last shuddering sigh she opened her eyes and looked into his face. His eyes glittered and he smiled an arrogantly male smile and she had to laugh.

"I suppose after a few hundred years of having sex you would be quite good at it," she said with a saucy grin.

He laughed. "Was that a compliment to my skills, love?"

"You've fucked me boneless, so yes, it's a definite compliment. I think I'll keep you since you're so well-trained."

"It's you. Part of it is skill, I'm pleased to say, but it's mainly you and I. It's never been this good, this intense with anyone else. I love you."

She rolled off him and kissed his neck. "I love you, too."

Afterwards, as they lay, legs entwined, under the covers he caressed the skin of her arms and kissed her shoulder, knowing that he would never be able to touch her enough to end the craving.

* * * * *

After they'd made love once more and showered they decided to grab some dinner. On the way out the door the phone rang.

"Hang on, I need to get that in case it's someone in my family," Lee called out as she reached for the phone.

"Okay, I'm going to run back to my apartment for a bit. Come and get me when you're finished," he said. She watched as he jogged up the stairs to his place. He looked as good going as he did coming. She closed her door with a sigh of pleasure and picked up the phone. "Hello?"

"Lee, I felt something happening to you. Something amazing and very important."

"*Tante* Elise, how are you?"

"Enough about me, what's happening?" Lee smiled, imagining her great-aunt's hand waving away her questions, urging her to get to the point of the call.

"Well, Aidan and I exchanged blood tonight, while we were together I just spoke these words, words I had no idea I even knew until I said them. They were from a binding ritual from his culture. He says that we're married, essentially."

"Ah, so that's what it was. I felt your souls meld together all the way over here. It's a good thing. He's good for you."

"So you aren't even going to lecture me on marrying a man I've known for a day?" Lee laughed.

"No, *cher*, you are the most grounded person I know. Mature, smart, responsible. If you are with him, you are meant to be. Bring him to dinner Sunday. Be well, my heart," *tante* Elise said and hung up.

Chuckling to herself, she locked up and walked upstairs to Aidan's. She supposed that now that they were married they should move in together, at least. She knocked and he opened the door, holding the phone to his ear. He motioned her inside.

"Get back to me as soon as you can, Da. I love you too." He hung up and went to her, embracing her from behind. "Sorry about that. They send their blessings and their love and wanted me to tell you they're anxious to meet you."

She turned and kissed his lips. She could feel the tension in his body, see the lines around his eyes. "Don't be. However, you do need to tell me whatever it was that made you sound so upset." She led him to the couch and pulled him to sit beside her.

"Oh that." He rubbed his eyes and then combed his fingers though his hair with some agitation. "Well, I knew that a pairing with a witch would be different in some ways, but I fear I should have done more homework before the binding. My father believes that since you are a witch, and because you took my blood during the binding, that I most likely started the conversion. I'm so sorry, I would never have done it without asking if I had known."

Even if she couldn't feel his upset, she could hear it in his voice. She felt totally sure that he'd never do anything so totally life-altering to her without speaking to her first and as such, it never entered her mind that he'd known about the outcome he felt so worried about.

Grabbing his hand from his hair she kissed the knuckles. "So why don't you tell me about conversion since it appears to be something that's happening."

"Conversion usually takes several exchanges, the last one kills the human cells, and then the vampire blood comes in and changes the DNA. It's a painful and not often successful process."

She looked shocked and raised her hands to her throat. "Are you telling me I'm going to die?"

He grabbed her hand in reassurance. "No! You won't, not at all. I was describing what the conversion with humans usually is so you can understand how I didn't know that I might have started the conversion with you."

"So, I'm going to turn into a vampire?"

"Well, yes. But not for a very long time and my father doesn't believe the change will be complete. He's going to do some research and get back to me. There have been matings between vampires and witches in the past and he's going to track a few of these coupled down to talk with them about it. I'm so sorry."

She mulled it over for a few minutes. "Well, I was very sad that I'd not have very long with you and that you'd stay young and I'd age and die. My *tante* Elise called and said she felt our bonding was a good thing and I agree with her. You didn't know. I appreciate that you would have asked me ahead of time but I would have agreed anyway. Are you disappointed not to be rid of me in forty or fifty years?"

He got to his knees in front of her and buried his face in her lap. She ran her hands through his hair. "Five hundred years with you sounds like heaven. I don't deserve you."

"Why would you say such a thing?"

"I don't deserve you because you have taken everything I've told you in stride, without any upset or agitation. Why are you so unafraid, so accepting?" Aidan asked, his heart full to bursting with love and adoration for this woman, *his* woman.

She shrugged. "I dunno. Seems to me there are things you can change and things you can't. When I saw you yesterday, I knew you were mine and I was yours. It was hard to grasp, thinking in general terms, but I've seen a lot of things in my lifetime that were hard to grasp and yet they were real. My family feels it's real. My heart and mind and power tell me what we have is real and I accept that. I could run from it, but the outcome would be the same and I'd be unhappy and causing you unhappiness in the meantime. Doesn't seem worth it.

"With the conversion stuff, again, I can't change it, it's happening. I will miss my siblings. That part, leaving behind humans that I love as they grow old and die, will be very hard, but what can I do but love and appreciate them while I have them around?"

"I love you, Lee," he said softly, his hands gliding up her thighs, pushing her skirt up around her waist.

"Hey, I'm sore and hungry! We can have more of that later," she said with a giggle as he tickled the back of her knee.

He pulled her panties slowly down and palmed her mound, slowly rotating his hand until she moaned and he felt her surrender. "I just need to taste you again. I'll be gentle and quick, I promise. And I'll get you dinner right away," he said with a murmur as he opened her thighs and placed them on his shoulders.

He leaned in and gave her a lick from her gate to her clit and back again, pleased that she was already juicy for him. He drank her in, nibbling and laving over her humid flesh. He loved nothing more than a woman's pussy all desire-soft and weeping for him. This pussy was clearly going to be an addiction, he knew that. This woman already was.

He slowly pushed two fingers inside of her and shivered to hear her moan, to feel her hips arching up to meet him. Her honey tasted sweet and tangy, she smelled like jasmine and lavender and vanilla, like sex and flowers. He let his incisors graze over her hard clit and gloried in her shivers of delight.

"Oh my god, what was that? Do it again! Oh yes. Aidan, yes." She moaned.

"I'm going to eat you up, pet," he growled and latched onto her distended clit, sucking it in and out of his mouth, fucking her with his fingers.

She trembled and began to whimper, then screamed, back bowing off the couch, flesh pressing into his face, riding his hand until she sighed and slumped back, legs weakly dropping off his shoulders.

He sat up and licked his fingers, giving her a wicked grin that foretold pleasures to come later on. He helped her back into her panties and raised an eyebrow, nodding in the direction of his bedroom.

"No!" she said weakly, standing up and straightening her skirt, her leg muscles trembling. "You are temptation personified but I am starving! You promised me food. I'll let you fuck me silly after we eat. Lots of times."

He chuckled. "Oh all right. We should discuss the living arrangements, too. I want to sleep next to you every day, but these apartments are too small for two people to have work spaces," he said, helping her to the door. "I also need to get you a ring. We should do a human wedding, too."

She smiled as they walked out of the door and down the steps. "That would be lovely but we don't have to if you don't want to." She felt a prickle at the base of her spine and looked up. A man was standing near the fountain. Lee froze and Aidan went on alert. The man was dangerous and he stank of dark magic.

"Miss Charvez? I'm Edmund DeGuerra. May I have a moment of your time?" He was tall and lean, skin and bones, really. His dark hair was cropped very close to his head, only succeeding in making his waterless blue eyes look even more spooky. He reminded her of someone out of a horror film and she nearly laughed at the odd thought, despite the danger.

"What's this all about?" Lee said, throwing up a wall of protection around her and Aidan.

"Protective spells are not necessary, Miss Charvez, or may I call you Amelia?"

"Ms. Charvez is fine. And I'll decide what is necessary." She wrinkled her nose with distaste as she looked him over physically and metaphysically. "The smell of your dark master is all over you. What do you want?"

"As you wish, of course," he said with an obsequious bow. "My employer, a man of great power, would like to meet with you and your family. The three living witch dreamers, that is."

"Why?" Lee's eyes narrowed at the tall, gaunt man.

"He is a curious man, he'd like to meet you. He'd also like to broker the terms of your surrender."

Lee laughed, the sound filling the courtyard. The air itself pulsated with the ripples moving outward from her. Aidan felt her power leave her body in a warm tide. He smiled as he saw DeGuerra's face fall and he moved back from her warily. DeGuerra lost some of his hauteur as he realized just how powerful Lee was.

"This is our town and your *boss* knows this. The Compact makes it so. Your boss is the interloper, it is he who needs to surrender before he is vanquished."

"You are making a mistake. He is, shall we say, fascinated with you, Miss Charvez, and feels that with you ruling at his side as his dark queen, much could happen."

Now it was Aidan's turn to laugh. "Ms. Charvez is taken. She is my mate, my wife."

"My master does not recognize your laws, vampire. Ms. Charvez is his to take," DeGuerra said with a sneer.

Aidan's incisors lengthened and he growled. Lee caressed his arm and gave a small shake of her head. "What your master believes is of no consequence to me. I am no pet to be owned or claimed," she stated calmly. "And your boss is who?" Lee asked imperiously, tossing in a spell of compulsion woven into the question.

"He is..." DeGuerra visibly had to work to get himself under control. After a few long moments he took a deep breath. "I am warded against compulsion spells, although yours is very good and I almost blurted it out." DeGuerra laughed and the sound made Lee's skin crawl. "I will leave his card here, on the edge of the fountain. It's an ordinary business card, no spells. Contact him when you admit you have no other choice." He turned and walked out of the courtyard.

"Damn it! I am destined to never get any dinner tonight," she said and stomped her foot. Not knowing if the card carried any harmful spells she closed her eyes and concentrated, projecting her power to the ledge of the fountain where the card lay.

She quickly memorized the number and then incinerated the card into less than ash. She laid a cleansing spell over the general area and returned back to herself.

"Well?" Aidan asked.

"Damian Cole is his name, or at least what he calls himself, I doubt he'd give us his true name. I'll call my mother on the way to their house. We need to tell them we're married now anyway. Since it's obvious we won't be going out to dinner, I can eat there. They've always got good leftovers," she said and he kissed her hand and followed her to the garage.

* * * * *

He drove so she could call and make arrangements. He gave a low whistle of appreciation when they pulled into the long driveway of the house on First Street.

"Wow, this is amazing. I love these old houses, there's something so classically American South about them all. I walked past this place on my walking tour. I can't believe you grew up here."

She smiled warmly and then looked at the house. The ivy-covered front walls, the columns, the ironwork. Her mother's roses were in full bloom, sending their heady fragrance out into the night. All these sights and smells were so intimately familiar to her that sometimes she forgot to see their beauty. "It is lovely, isn't it? It's been in the family for generations now. It'll be mine someday. Technically, it's mine now but I have no desire to kick my parents out, even though we will need to look for a bigger place to live."

"Lee, I suppose I should tell you that I'm quite wealthy. We'll buy our own house."

She turned and gave him a smile. "Oh, thank you. I guess it won't go oldest daughter to oldest daughter, since we can't have kids," she said and he caught the wistfulness in her tone. "But Em will have children, perhaps it will go to one of her daughters."

"Ah, well, about that. If you are going through the conversion, at some point there will be a chance of procreation. My mother was young, in relative terms, when she had me. She'd only been a vampire for about twenty years, and she was twenty when she went through conversion. Newly converted vampire females are still fertile for the first eighty to one hundred years. It's the lingering human fertility, apparently, that makes it possible. It will be a joy to see what sort of mixture the child of a witch dreamer and a vampire will be." He smiled as he imagined a daughter with gorgeous auburn curls and her mother's violet eyes.

"So I could be pregnant now?" she squeaked and he laughed and squeezed her hand and got out to help her out of the car.

"Probably not, you've only just begun the conversion but if you don't want to be right now, you should go on the pill or I can use condoms, whichever you prefer."

"I'll go on the pill. I like the way you feel inside of me without a condom. I love the idea of having children with you but there's a lot of bad stuff going on right now and I'm just learning to harness my power. I think the timing is wrong."

"Good idea, but I just want to say that any time you want to have our children is fine with me," he said, kissing her lightly as they walked hand in hand up the stairs to the front door.

Her father opened it and gave Aidan a long, assessing look. Lee stepped in between them and gave her father a glare. "Daddy, stop that. Emile Broussard, this is Aidan Bell. Aidan, this is my father."

Aidan held out his hand and her father took it, shaking it and inviting them inside. "Go on through to the dining room. Your momma's got some food laid out for you. Georgie made shrimp salad for dinner."

She walked in and bent to kiss her mother's cheeks. "*Maman*, this is Aidan Bell. Aidan, this is my mother, Marie Charvez."

Aidan took her hand and kissed it, bowing slightly. "My pleasure. I see where Lee gets her good looks."

Her mother quirked up the corners of her mouth. "I like this one, you can keep him." She looked back to Lee, motioning them to the table. "Sit and eat, you got some things to tell me," she said and they sat and filled their plates.

"Well, first and foremost, Aidan and I are married. We performed the binding ritual of his culture tonight and we plan on having a human ceremony as soon as we can."

"You what!" her father thundered and stood up, starting to pace. Lee and her mother simply looked up and him and smiled, knowing his protective instincts were on full alert, and went back to eating. "Lee, sug, you married a vampire? Honey, after knowing him one day?"

Lee looked up at him and smiled patiently. The men who were related to the Charvez women had a huge cross to bear. Charvez women were notoriously independent and headstrong, they were powerful and while young, like most kids, they had more power than sense. It was difficult for Emile to reconcile the woman before him with his baby girl. He wanted her to be happy, he knew she was a smart woman with a big helping of common sense, but at the same time, she was still his little girl and she'd brought home a vampire that she'd met the day before. He wanted to protect her, even though he knew she was more than capable of protecting herself.

"Daddy, it is simply meant to be. Em read him, *grandmere* and *tante* Elise have declared him to be the right man for me, the man I'm meant to be with. I love him and he loves me. I know it's odd and hard to accept but some things are simply fated to be. Now sit down before Aidan thinks you don't like him."

Aidan watched with concealed amusement as Lee's father sat back down and her mother reached out for his hand and patted it gently. He looked at his wife and repeated, "He's a vampire."

Aidan decided to step in. "Yes, sir, I am. Part of your concern is most likely based on the negative folklore that surrounds my kind. Please let me assure you that very little of it is true. Our hearts beat, we have souls and while we do need blood to live, we don't take it from the unwilling. I would never harm anyone in anything other than self-defense or in the defense of someone I love. I can go inside of churches, and crosses do not repel me at all. I would give my very life to protect your daughter, she is my everything."

The smile Lee sent to Aidan was full of love and adoration and Emile saw it and understood. "He is no threat to us, Daddy. He's a good person with a good heart and he makes me happy. Isn't that what you have always told me you wanted for me in a husband? His parents gave their blessing, can't you do the same? Please?" She blinked up at her father and Aidan realized that no man in his right mind would be able to refuse this woman anything she asked for.

"Parents?" Her father looked confused.

"Yes sir, both my parents live in Ireland but they will come over to meet Lee very soon. My father has a highly respected position in our government. He's a great scholar and leader. He's finishing up a project at the moment but they will come when he's finished. My grandmother lives in Chicago. I haven't told her about the binding yet, but I did tell her that I'd met Lee and I know we'll all be arranging to meet soon."

"Well, it's not as if our family is normal either, I suppose," her father said. "Okay, baby, I'm glad you're happy, if he makes you that way, you have my blessing. Just see you do, young man, and you'd do fine to call me Emile."

"He's two hundred and forty-five years old, Dad." Lee laughed at the idea of her father calling Aidan, "young man".

"Shh! Just let me have a few illusions please, darling," her father said gruffly and Lee hugged him tightly, kissing his forehead.

"We will begin to plan the wedding soon. I'll want to get your mother's number, Aidan, so that I can include her," Lee's mother said. "Now that you're married, Lee, it's time for me and your *papa* to move out and let you take over here, it's your legacy."

Lee shook her head vehemently and refused. She wanted something of her own for a while, something that was hers and Aidan's. If she moved into the Charvez house, everyone in the family would feel free to drop over at any time. Aside from that, her parents were still young and Lee had no intention of displacing them. "Aidan and I will look for a place, most likely out this way," she said finally, refusing to discuss it further.

Her mother sighed heavily and tapped Lee's hand. "Now, you have something else to tell me."

Lee told her mother about DeGuerra and the business card she had destroyed. They discussed the name he'd given and pretty much decided that it would be a fake. Real names had power and it would be rare and stupid for him to have exposed himself in that way.

"Wants our terms of surrender does he? Pompous ass," her mother huffed and then went off on a long invective in French.

"We should have Eric run the name and number through the computer and see what he can dig up," Lee said as she pushed her plate away and sat back. Eric was an attorney at her father's firm and he would have access to searchable databases to run records checks. "After we've warded his office, or maybe he can do the work here. I don't want him in danger."

Chapter Four

"Let's go for a walk. The night air smells so good," Aidan said as they walked out of the house. Hand in hand, they slowly walked the blocks of the Garden District, feeling the power course through the air. She gave him a mini-tour of the area, pointing out the different sights. Aidan loved getting to know her, the little things, the way her head tilted when she spoke, how her eyes sparkled when she talked about her family, the way she had to move her hands when she spoke.

They turned down a last block to make the circuit back to the car and there stood a house with a "For Sale" sign out front. Lee felt like a hand had grabbed the back of her clothing and pulled her to a halt. The house was simply beautiful. A Greek Revival style home with columns and wraparound porches on both stories, it was nothing out of the ordinary to the naked eye, it was even a bit run-down-looking, but it pulsed with life. As they stood on the sidewalk and looked at it, Lee felt a tug on her heart and soul. The house felt like home, like it was calling to her.

They walked through the wrought iron gate and up the paved walkway, and it was as if she'd wiped a wet cloth over a dirty window. The house was vibrant, teeming with color and beauty. It was like she'd sensed it from the corner of her eye outside of the gate but once inside, the glamour had fallen away and the true house showed itself to them.

Seeing that the house was empty, they walked through the willows and magnolia trees, smelling the sweet scent of flowers and earth. Around the back they walked up onto the grand porch and approached the door. She imagined some chairs and a glider swing there, sitting out in the evenings, watching the stars with Aidan. Lee could see their children playing in the large willow tree, a big tire swing that they'd put up.

Lee put her hand on the doorknob of the back door, trying to remember the unlock spell her *tante* Elise had taught her as a child, but before she could speak the words, the knob turned easily under her hand as if the house was inviting them inside.

Once inside, they walked around from room to room. Lee devoured each detail of the house with her eyes. The craftsmanship was exquisite, the woodworking on the moldings was delicate and intricate and linked to the overall design theme in the stained glasswork and the tiling. Fine vines and flowers bloomed in the deep walnut and cherry wood, and in the glass of the house. It was then that Lee realized that it was after ten at night and she was seeing all of the fine design work in the dark.

Amazed, she mentioned it to Aidan.

"It's the conversion. We have excellent night vision," Aidan said as they walked up the gleaming, ornately carved wooden staircase that curved with the grace of a woman's body. It seemed unthinkable that the house had been empty for any length of time, it simply spoke of being loved, of having inhabitants that spent a great deal of time with their hands on it. The notion wasn't hard to grasp, every surface called out to be touched, to be caressed.

"This house is something special. It calls to me," Lee whispered.

"Yes, it's meant to be ours. One sense that vampires most definitely possess is knowing when a place is safe for us. This house feels that way. Plenty of room for both of us to have studios. The master suite is huge and the light can easily be shut out when I need to sleep. The yard is big, the house well off the street so we'd have privacy. It's close to your parents but not too close."

Lee's heart felt lighter for the decision to own the house, or to rather to love the house—it almost felt like a live thing. She nodded and kissed the hand she was holding. "I'll call the realtor first thing. This house is bound to be expensive but I have money in savings that can go toward a down payment."

Aidan pulled her to him. "Baby, this will be my gift to you. As I told you earlier, I'm quite wealthy. Two hundred and forty-five years on this earth can really aid in building up stock portfolios."

"I don't know, Aidan, I don't want you to feel responsible for me. I can pay my own way."

"Lee, your own way is apparently saving New Orleans from evildoers. I have the money, what's mine is yours. If you had it and I didn't, wouldn't you do the same thing?"

She smirked at him and nodded reluctantly. He told her he'd speak to his man of business and arrange for her to be given access to his accounts so that she could handle the transfer of any funds necessary.

They walked through the house one last time before slowly strolling to the car and driving back home.

"So, I hope you don't think I'll be sleeping alone tonight," he said with that wickedly sensual smile she'd come to love.

She gave him an arched eyebrow. "Well, you don't sleep at night anyway."

He chuckled, deliberately sending out that sex mojo that he did with his voice.

"You don't play fair." She gave him a pretty pout.

"But I play to win. I promise to make it worth your while if you stay at my place."

"Well," she sighed dramatically, "I suppose that since you'd be absolutely no good to me if you got harmed by the sun in my non-vampire-proofed apartment, we can stay at your place until we get into our house."

She packed some of her clothes and it made him happy to see them around his place, her clothes in his closet, her toothbrush next to his, her scent on his couch. Soon to be in his bed.

At midnight she quit sketching and took a long shower and when she walked out of the bathroom he was waiting for her, stretched out on the bed, wearing nothing more than a smile.

"I came to tuck you in," he said in a low, sexy baritone that made her shiver in anticipation.

"Make it worth my while," she challenged.

He pulled her to him and brought his lips down on hers. He feathered his tongue over the seam of her lips and she opened to him and sucked it into her mouth. Her taste rushed through his system like a drug and that fast his body was screaming to take her, pushing his control to the limit. He adjusted her so that his cock was bumping the notch between her legs, hardness to softness. He could feel the heat from her pussy through the fabric of her panties. He tortured them both by grinding himself against her, a rush of sensation but not quite enough.

Growling, he pushed her back on the bed and gave in to temptation as he tore off her tank top and panties. He covered her breasts with his hands, palming the nipples. She held her bottom lip between her teeth as she panted, eyes sliding closed against the intensity of her desire. He scented her desire and gave her a naughty grin as he continued the roll and pull rhythm of his hands at her nipples and kissed down her body.

He scooted down to the end of the bed and took a foot in his hands. He kneaded it and she groaned at how good it felt. Smiling, he gently bit down on the flesh of her arch and licked around her ankles. He repeated the movements on the other foot, kissing and nibbling up first one calf and then the other. He paid particular attention to the back of her knees, which had her alternating between sobbing with laughter and sobbing with desire.

When he finally reached her pussy and buried his face between her thighs, she gave a mewl of pleasure. "Mmmm. Oh yesss. Right there," she said and arched up. He parted her with his hands and lapped at her, slurping her clit and tonguing her gate. He pushed his face deep into the folds of her pussy and she squealed in delight. He drank of her greedily, not wanting to miss a drop of her tangy honey. He wanted to give her as much pleasure as she'd given him the last time they were together. He kept building her up, suckling her distended clit, fucking her with his fingers, then backing off a few beats until she'd leveled off again, only to come back and work to bring her up again.

"Oh god," she moaned and he started to pull back but she grabbed his head and kept his face to her flesh. "Don't stop," she ordered and he laughed and scraped his teeth gently over her clit and she jumped and screamed as she gushed cream and came. He pressed his face to her flesh, taking in every bit of her honey that he could.

"You taste so good," he said as she sat up.

She turned to him and licked a path across his chest. His skin heated at her touch. She pushed him back against the mattress and knelt between his thighs, her auburn curls like silk over his naked skin as she kissed and licked her way down his body. He cried out when she bit the flesh around his nipple, just until it began to hurt, then pulled back and laved the sting with her tongue.

He pushed her back and stood up. Unwrapping a condom and rolling it on quickly, he growled out, "I need to fuck you right now." Taking her hands, he brought her forward and using his vampire strength, picked her up and she wrapped her legs around his waist. He adjusted her position and surged up while his hands at her waist plunged her down, both of them yelling out as his cock sliced through her hot sheath. She arched and tightened around him and he lost his ability to breathe for a few moments.

"Oh please, Aidan. Move. Fuck me," she whispered in his ear and he took in a breath, his chest expanding like a bellows, and began to thrust inside of her, dragging almost completely out and slamming back in. She whimpered and begged and moaned.

"I want to see you come again, Lee, I want to feel your sweet pussy milk me. Can you do that for me, baby?" he whispered in her ear and she shivered. He put a hand to her lips and she sucked his thumb inside, biting it and swirling her tongue around it. He looked at her, eyes glittering with greedy lust, and pulled his moistened thumb free and found her clit with it, moving it slowly, methodically over her swollen flesh.

"Ohhhh yessss," she hissed and he felt her climax hit, watched her nipples darken and get even harder, felt the walls of her sheath pulse and flutter around him as he slammed into her over and over, mindless to anything but the way her pussy sucked at his cock, refusing to let it leave her body.

When he came the pleasure shot through his body like a lightning bolt. His head fell back and he felt her fingernails pierce the skin at his shoulder, the pain putting a fine edge on the pleasure of coming inside of her.

He stumbled over to the bed and sat down, still hard and embedded deeply within her. He felt his incisors lengthen and he looked at her, asking without words for permission to taste her.

"Please," she moaned and he moved them both back so he could sit up against the headboard. Her head lolled back, her body arched toward him. She continued to ride him in a dreamy rhythm. He dragged his incisors across the spot on her left breast that he'd used before.

She gave a deep, guttural groan as she began to climax around him, her hands on his shoulders, holding him to her tightly. "Yes, take from me," she whispered hoarsely and he sat back up, only taking the tiniest of tastes from her veins, and found himself unbelievably right on the edge of his own orgasm. He brought his wrist to his mouth and opened a vein there. Holding it to her mouth she leaned in and gingerly at first, touched her lips to his flesh and then with a sigh, held him tighter and drank him in. At the brush of her lips he cried out, grabbing her hip with his free hand, emptying himself into her, his cock pulsing with the beat of his heart. She moaned as she pulled back, licking her lips, and he quickly closed the wound and kissed her hard, this mate of his who lived in his world without any hesitation or fear. Her tongue slid over his and she sucked his into her mouth. His incisors were retracting and she flicked her tongue across them and pushed him into a climax he never had thought possible, pleasure arced through his body in waves so big he felt as if he were drowning. After what seemed like years he lay down with her, her body tight against his after quickly disposing of the condom.

He realized then that he'd never ever get enough of her. That he wanted her so much he ached with it. She was everything to him and he understood what his parents had and felt so fortunate to have it for his own.

"You *are* a witch. One touch of your tongue on my incisors and you brought me off less than two minutes after I came the *second* time. That was incredible."

She smiled that sexy smile of hers and his cock gave a twitch of interest. He groaned out a laugh. "Yeah, it was, wasn't it?" She said dreamily, "I love you." She snuggled against him. He felt her slip away into sleep just moments later.

* * * * *

Aidan felt so sated, so relaxed and happy that he worked in his studio until nearly seven the next morning. Before he went to bed, he showered and called Alex, his best friend in Chicago, to tell him about Lee and to seek his input on the situation with the dark power.

"Carter," Alex barked into the phone. In addition to being a powerful wizard, Alex was also a highly successful broker. By that time of the morning he would have been at work for two hours, at least.

"Hey, man, how's the market today?"

"For you, always good, you rich bastard. How goes New Orleans?"

"Excellent. I found her, my dream woman. She's real, Alex. I shouldn't have doubted my gran." He chuckled. "We got married yesterday, said the binding. We've decided to do the human ceremony soon and I'll be expecting you to stand up for me."

"Jeez, I didn't think you'd find her so quickly, you've only been in New Orleans for a few weeks! Congratulations! She must be something else. I take it she knows what you are and is okay with it?"

Aidan laughed. "Lee is indeed something else. Yes, she not only knows what I am but didn't even bat an eye at it. She's utterly fearless, Alex. She's beautiful, about five and a half feet, wild and curly auburn hair, violet eyes. She moves with this amazing grace. The accent is a killer too. Oh, and she's a witch, a witch dreamer, to be exact."

"A witch dreamer? They're rare, Aidan. A Charvez, right? I don't know much, wizards don't think that highly of witches so my education isn't that detailed about them but I do know that they're powerful women."

"Tell me about it. There's something here, something bad and evil. She's fought it off twice now."

"Aidan, your witch, does she have a dimple on her left cheek?"

"Yeah, every time I see it I want to eat her up."

"Does she wear an amulet, silver? Looks like three sevens, stylized to curve into a circle?"

"Yes, she does. Alex, how did you know that?"

Alex sighed and Aidan heard his friend's hesitation.

"Alex?"

"I've dreamed of her. Only once, a waking dream."

Aidan looked up and watched Lee begin to stir. She sat up, her hair tousled around her face, sheet falling away from her naked body. She caught him looking at her and mouthed *good morning* to him as she got up and padded into the bathroom.

"Aid, you pissed at me?" Alex asked.

"Huh?" Aidan came back to himself and his phone call. He had to force himself away from thinking about Lee and how beautifully tousled she'd looked. "Pissed? No, why would I be? You had a dream of her, it's not like you did it on purpose. But it must mean something. What was it about?"

"Well, if she's a witch dreamer she most likely had the same waking dream that I did. It might have been slightly different, because she'd be seeing it from her perspective, but the event would have been the same. It wasn't overly detailed or long. There was a circuit of power being formed. I don't know much more that that. I probably should have called you yesterday when it happened but sometimes dreams are meaningful, sometimes they're not. I was going to call your grandmother today."

"Hmm. Interesting. I'll ask her about it. She just woke up."

"Ah, that's why you got all distracted," Alex said in a teasing voice.

"Yeah, she looks pretty darned good walking naked across my apartment." He heard the shower turn on. "Speaking of that, we're going to be buying a house. I think we found the one last night, big enough to accommodate a guest when you come for the wedding and other visits."

Alex laughed. "You've got it, I wouldn't dream of being anywhere else when you marry Lee, I can't wait to meet her. I've got to go, the market is all over the place this morning. I'll talk to you later. I'm really happy for you, man."

"Ta. Have a good one," he said and hung up, tossing off his clothes as he hurried toward the bathroom, tapping on the door and going inside.

"I was wondering when you'd come and visit me," she said from behind the curtain. He stepped into the tub with her and rubbed against her soap-slick skin like a cat. "Mmmm. Morning," she said as he bent to kiss her.

"I like this morning the best of all," he said as he picked her up and she wrapped her legs around him. "Damn it, I used my last condom last night," he said with regret, his fingers curved around her thighs, the tips stroking over her pussy. He gave a smirk of male arrogance when he found her wet and she rolled her eyes.

"It's the wrong time of the month for me to get pregnant anyway. I'm going to call my doctor's office when they open to see if they can renew my old birth control prescription, if not I'll have to go in to see her. In any case, it takes a few weeks before it's effective again so I'll grab some condoms while I'm out."

"Renew your prescription?"

She laughed. "You think I was a virgin until yesterday? I'm twenty-seven years old."

"Hmph," he said, positioning the head of his cock just inside of her. He was still for a moment and then surged inside of her completely, causing her to gasp and arch into him. "I'll erase all others from your head."

"You already have," she whispered into his ear.

After their shower she dressed in the clothes she'd brought up the night before and ate some toast and had a cup of coffee. She'd discovered to her dismay that he didn't drink coffee. "Honestly, I don't know if I would have married you if I'd known you weren't a big coffee person."

He laughed and gave a big yawn. "I forgot to ask you this earlier but have you had any dreams lately with a dark-haired man in them?"

"Oh my god! I totally forgot to tell you. In the midst of all of the excitement with Lurch's visit and the house it slipped my mind, well, that and your face between my thighs." She gave him a wry grin.

She sipped her coffee and took a bite from her toast. "I did have a waking dream yesterday afternoon. It was odd, so vivid. I rarely have waking dreams. My magic dreams usually come when I'm unconscious. Anyway—" she waved her hand at him, "—there was a dark-haired man with leaf green eyes. He was holding his hand out to me, I could feel that he wanted to protect me. He was wary but when I grabbed his hand I felt something shift inside of me, like a final piece had been put in a puzzle. I don't know him though. You were there, too, and you were smiling at both me and the other man."

"It's Alex. My friend, the wizard from Chicago. I talked to him this morning. He had the same dream yesterday afternoon."

Aidan felt a stab of jealousy, a bit of fear mixed with the curiosity. Why was Lee dreaming of Alex? What did it mean? Why was Alex so weird about it on the phone with him earlier?

"I brought it up to my *grandmere*, she said it was important-that three was important. He's supposed to be with us here. I didn't know it was your friend, I suppose that makes things easier, we now know who is supposed to come when the time is right. Damn, she's good. I may be able to toss around balls of flame but she's amazing. What did Alex say about it?"

"First things first, he's supposed to be with us how?"

"I don't know. It was just a short dream. I'll have more and it will come to me, or he'll come here and we'll all figure it out," she said, kissing him. "Aidan, are you all right? You seem agitated." She pushed her chair closer to his and touched his hand.

He nodded slowly. "I think so. It's just odd to have your wife dreaming about another man and to have that other man dream about her too, especially when you and I dreamed of each other."

Her face was etched with concern. "Aidan, the kind of dream I had about you was different than the one I had about Alex. In my dreams of you, we were together, naked sweaty together, walking hand in hand together, *together* together. They were magic dreams, I like to think of them as fate dreams.

"The waking dream I had of Alex yesterday was more metaphorical than anything else. I don't have them very often, as I said, but I can tell you that all it was, was a flash of a moment with the three of us. You were there and you weren't upset, you were smiling." She saw his discomfort and she wanted to allay his concerns but it was hard to put into words. Magic was something that she just did, that she'd dealt with her whole life and now she had to explain it to his satisfaction and she wasn't quite sure if she could completely explain his fears away.

He relaxed a bit but was still worried for both his best friend and his woman. "Okay, love. Don't you forget those condoms, I plan to have my wicked way with you when I wake up tonight. Several times." He waggled his eyebrows and she laughed.

"Go to bed, you look tired. I'm going downstairs to call my doctor and the realtor. I'm going to work in the shop today after my training session with *maman* and *tante* Elise. I'll be home at about six."

"If you get home early, come crawl into bed with me," he said, pulling her into a hug.

"Your wish is my command." And with a last wave, she headed out to start her day.

* * * * *

Because Lee's old prescription was still valid, she was able to stop by her doctor's office and pick up her pills, but she also picked up a jumbo box of condoms at the pharmacy. The teenaged boy behind the counter blushed when he rang them up. She held back a grin.

As she walked into the shop, her sister, Em, leaped at her and enveloped her into a hug. "Congratulations, sug! *Maman* said that you got married to that handsome Aidan. I can't believe you didn't call me!"

Lee laughed at her younger sister's effusive reaction. Em was pretty shy around most people but in those rare moments that she showed that total joy, she glowed with it and Lee wished she saw her sister that way more often.

"It just happened last night, it wasn't planned or anything. I do want you to be my maid of honor at the wedding, though. We'll be doing that sometime soon."

"You're forgiven, but only if you don't make me wear something stupid. Does Aidan have any brothers?"

Laughing, Lee put in a call to the realtor and made an offer on the house, he said he'd call her back when he'd contacted the seller. She made herbal tea infusions with Em and they laughed with their aunt as they watched her create bundles of healing herb mixtures.

After her training session, the realtor called back and told her that the offer had been accepted on the house. She and Em drove over to the realtor's office and signed the papers and Lee gave him a check for the earnest money. They explained that Aidan's job made it difficult to get away during the day and that he would sign the papers and have them returned back to the office first thing the next morning.

He looked puzzled. "Funny thing about that house, it's been on the market for two years. I know it's a bit run-down, but in that part of town we don't usually have a property empty for more than a few weeks."

Lee smiled, the house wasn't run-down at all, it had just been waiting to be found.

* * * * *

She and Aidan fell into a routine over the next week. She worked in her apartment and slept at his. She hadn't had any more waking dreams of Alex and, on the advice of her *grandmere*, anxiously waited to see what her next step should be.

Lee continued to train with her mother and her great-aunt. She realized just how much she had to learn and how very powerful and talented the other two women were.

"I thought you said I was the most powerful witch dreamer in generations," she said exhaustedly as she collapsed into a chair after her mother had made her work on the same failed spell over and over again for three hours straight until she finally got it right.

"You have the power, Lee, but you don't know how to wield it, not the full extent of it in any case. It's more than just possessing the power, it's knowing what to do with it." Her mother raised a brow at her.

"We don't know what this Damian Cole is up to. Until we do, you must continue to hone your skills or I fear you will not be able to stand against him," *tante* Elise said.

She sighed and nodded, taking a drink of her iced tea and getting back to work.

Chapter Five

A week after they'd started escrow on the house, her mother rushed into the shop, looking pale, breathing hard. Lee rushed to her and grabbed her hand. "*Maman*! What is it?" she asked, alarmed.

"I have walked this morning, *cher*. This new power in town, he is a sorcerer, a master of the black arts. He is a death wielder."

"No," *tante* Elise breathed out. "Oh this changes things. I felt the evil, the stench of his presence, but...you are sure?"

"I went walking, I ended up in his subconscious. I saw the ritual."

"*Maman*, *tante* Elise, what is a death wielder?" Lee asked, turning and pouring a glass of the iced herbal tea that was always available at the shop and handing it to her mother.

"You know that our power is inherent, yes? That we are born with natural gifts?" her aunt asked and Lee nodded. "Well, the Charvez witches' power comes from the elements, from the very earth herself.

"There are also wizards like your Aidan's friend, Alex, who practice a more arcane magic. They are not always good and not always evil. Their power is also inherent.

"Lastly, we have dark mages whose power comes from making deals with the less-than-wholesome elements of the universe — blood magic, sacrifices, and trucking with dark forces. A death wielder is strong, very strong, because he gains his power through the death of others and the relinquishing of souls to a demon lord." She shuddered and drew a sigil in the air.

"This death wielder wants you, Lee. I do not feel that your apartment is safe enough to stand against him, even with the warding. You must move to somewhere with more magical protection right away. You can come back home," her mother said.

"If you think so, I'll do it today. Aidan is still resting though, I can't leave without him. I get that he's a bad guy and all but why is it suddenly so much more serious that I have to move?"

"To have you, the strongest witch dreamer in generations, at his side would cement his position. If he was able to corrupt your power the results would be catastrophic. The Compact could be in jeopardy," *tante* Elise added.

"The Compact? So tell me how his involvement puts the Compact in danger. I understand how it would affect me personally, but how can that break the promise that was made generations ago?" Lee looked to her mother, wishing that she'd known about the Compact for longer than a week.

"Nothing is perfect, even when made by a nearly perfect being like the angel who crafted the Compact. If the demon lord who agreed to the Compact can find a strong enough dark mage, that dark mage could try and break the Compact by breaking the strongest of the Charvez witches. That's you. If this dark mage was able to get to you, to corrupt your power or to kill you, this could happen."

"His lackey said he wanted me to rule as his dark queen…" Lee started to answer her mother when a waking dream descended into her consciousness, shoving everything else aside.

Suddenly she was standing in a warehouse. It was cold, the concrete beneath her feet bled a numbing chill through and up her legs. Her heart was pounding, she was afraid and angry. The rage she felt washed over her and made her breath hitch. She turned and saw Aidan, he reached out and took her hand and she felt the warmth of his power flow from him into her, slowly. She turned her head and saw the dark-haired man. He held out his hand and she joined hers with it and a blinding white light exploded through her system as the three of them shared their magic, their elemental power and suddenly, through the anger and the fear, a sense of calm took over, creating a sharp focus.

The warehouse was humming with their combined energies, she felt it in her teeth. They aimed their power outward in a shock of light.

"Lee!" her sister was yelling, running her hands up and down Lee's arms.

Lee blinked her eyes, slowly coming back to herself. She was flushed, her hands and feet were tingling and her hair felt staticky. She struggled to talk but she had cotton mouth. She'd never had a waking dream so intense. She could still feel the cold in her feet, even though it was at least ninety degrees outside. Finally finding her voice she managed to croak, "It's all right, it was a waking dream. It was Aidan's friend again. In my vision, he was joined with me, we melded our power, there was a blinding white light and Aidan had my hand, he was feeding me his power."

"Well, we knew he had something to do with this. Where is this friend?" her aunt asked.

"He lives in Chicago."

"We know now that he needs to come here, he's going to be instrumental in defeating this death wielder. He needs to come," her mother repeated, desperation in her voice. "Tell him, Lee."

"All right, I need to arrange for a place to stay first if you think I should move," Lee said. "I wonder if they'd let us rent the house until escrow closes?" she wondered aloud and picked up the phone. The realtor told her he'd get back to her when he got an answer.

"Being so close to Lafayette, I could draw on all of that power to ward the house much more strongly than my apartment."

"This house, it's on Laurel?" *Tante* Elise asked. "Big stained glass panels in the entry?"

"Yes. You know it?" Lee asked.

"The house belonged to a very powerful psychic and her husband, who was a witch. He built it for her. My mother often spoke of it, and them. It would be the ideal place for you to live, my guess is that it will repel dark things and pull in the light," *tante* Elise said thoughtfully.

"Ah yes, the couple that lived there warded it, the very ground the house sits on, the paint, the glass, even the wrought iron fence," *tante* Elise added. "You were meant to find this house, *ange*."

"That's what it felt like."

The realtor called back within half an hour and told her that the seller, the granddaughter of the original builder, was willing to rent if they would agree to close in twenty-one days, which was agreeable to Lee and she was sure Aidan too.

Once they'd gotten the go-ahead and picked up the keys, Lee and her mother, grandmother, cousins and great-aunt went to the house to walk through it and ward if necessary. As they walked in through the gate in front they all stopped and breathed in deeply.

"Even here in the yard you can feel it. This house is a magical stronghold. Let's go inside." *Tante* Elise led the way as they walked through the house, testing each room, every wall and window, the attic and the flooring.

"This house, she will keep you and your man safe. Even that filth cannot get in. You see the pattern on that stained glass? It's got runes worked into the pattern, the same pattern is in the tile in the kitchen and the wallpaper in the hallways." *Tante* Elise looked around, satisfied that her grand-niece would be safe from the death wielder there.

"I can't believe I've never seen this place before," Lee's mother said as she brushed her fingertips over the carved wood of the banister.

"You weren't meant to. This house has been waiting for Lee, can't you feel that?" *Grandmere* said as she squeezed Lee's hand.

"Yes. You can visit any time, or stay, come to that. Will everyone else be safe? What about you, *maman*? Or *tante* Elise and the rest?"

"My dream...he wants you, *ange*. The First Street house has strong wards, as do the shop and *Tante* Elise's. The girls might want to stay in the apartments above the shop for a while or at our house, but I don't sense the threat around them," her mother said.

"I worry that if he can't get to me, he'll try to get to someone I love to get to me."

"Yes, I see, that is a good point. Em, darling, come and stay with me and *papa*, yes? And you too, Simone. We have so much room," Lee's mother said and her sister and cousin agreed.

It was late afternoon when they trooped to Lee's place and packed her up, her father and brothers taking the afternoon off to take the boxes over to the house in loads.

"I need to go upstairs to talk to Aidan. It's sunset in about half an hour, he should be awake or just waking up," she called out as she left the apartment, leaving them to continue packing.

She let herself into Aidan's apartment and felt him start to stir, his consciousness reaching out to hers. He got up quickly and came out to her, pulling her into his arms. "Baby, what is it? You're distressed."

She gave him an overview and he sat down with a sigh. "Well, I am relieved to hear our new home is so safe. We just need to get my window coverings set up in the bedroom to make sure it's tight against the daylight. I'd like to get my studio moved, and my clothes. The rest isn't absolutely imperative, it can happen tomorrow and over the next few days."

"Another thing," she hesitated. "Your friend Alex, he is important to this somehow, as I said last week, but we didn't really know how or why. I had another waking dream and he was in it. We had joined together and you were there too, feeding me power. I need to talk to him."

That vaguely uncomfortable feeling was there again. He shoved it away. "Okay, you know he's number two on my speed dial. Let me get dressed so that we can start packing my stuff up and you can call him. He may be home by now."

"First, are you hungry?" she asked softly, her voice low and smoky.

"I would wait until we are able to crawl into bed in our home together. I can take blood from you without sex, but I like the whole package much better. I am quite well-nourished from our interlude earlier, I can wait," he said with a grin and kissed her long and hard and went to get dressed.

She called her mother and sister up and they started packing the clothes while Lee went into the kitchen to call Alex.

"Carter," a voice answered and Lee felt it slide through her brain. It gave her a moment's pause.

"Is this Alex?" she asked.

He hesitated, knowing her immediately. "It's you," he said softly. "Amelia, the witch dreamer. Did you dream of me today?"

"Yes. You?"

"Yes. I've bought a plane ticket and am coming down tomorrow afternoon. I was planning to call Aidan in an hour or so to let him know."

"I'll pick you up at the airport," she said, memorizing his flight information. "You'll stay with us, of course, in our new home."

"Yes, thank you. Will you be safe?" he asked her, already feeling some odd sort of protectiveness toward his best friend's woman.

"Yes. You need to be safe as well. I don't want to get into specifics right now, but I assume you know how to guard yourself, yes?"

"Of course."

Aidan walked in and kissed the top of her head. She looked up at him, "Alex is flying in tomorrow afternoon, I'll pick him up at the airport."

She saw a flash of something in Aidan's eyes but it was gone as quick as it came. "Great! Did you tell him to plan on staying with us?"

"Yes, hang on." She turned her attention back to Alex. "I will see you tomorrow, Alex. Let me put Aidan on."

She handed the phone to Aidan and went into the other room to help pack his stuff up.

Aidan finished his call and some minutes later, walked into the room where Lee and the others were busily boxing up his belongings. He kissed her temple and tried not to think about the general uneasiness he felt about Alex's visit. Alex was his best friend, he was as close to the man as he would be to a brother. They'd shared a lot of things in the last fifteen years but he couldn't help but wonder just what Lee's dreams of him meant. He wasn't empathic but he could certainly hear the undisguised interest in Alex's voice when he spoke of Lee, the yearning in his responses when Aidan told him about his daily life with his wife. It also hadn't escaped his notice that the whole "triad" idea was about three and he wondered just how far this was going to go. He supposed that if he was honest about it, there was a bit of curiosity there as well as jealousy, and fear. Realizing all he could do was wait and see, he kissed Lee's temple one last time and got down to helping with the packing.

* * * * *

Alex Carter stood at the floor to ceiling windows looking out over the lake as he sipped his Scotch. He'd been listening to Aidan talk about his wife pretty much daily over the last week, and before that, his friend had talked about the dreams. Alex had been alone for most of his life, surrounded by people but feeling unconnected to them. Aidan had been one of the few people in his life who got him, who understood and accepted him for what he was instead of what he could do for him.

Alex envied Aidan's bond with Lee, envied that state of belonging to another person, that level of commitment. It was something he'd ached for for a long time but had accepted that he'd never have. And now he was mentally dallying with a woman who belonged to a man who was the brother of his heart—and he couldn't stop.

Lee's voice had wrapped around his head and he couldn't shake it. The softness of her accent, the lilt of her words, it made her physical to him, tangible. He couldn't get past his hunger to hear it again, wished she'd left a message on his voicemail so he could have listened to it again and again. He replayed the waking dreams in his head, imagining her face, the grace of her smile, the color of her eyes, the way her hand felt gripped in his own, how she trusted him.

He put his glass down and ran his palms down his thighs and back up, skating over the bulge at the juncture of his thighs. He imagined what she'd look like beneath him, that spill of curly red hair spread out wildly around her face as he fucked her hard and fast. He could feel the silky glide of the skin on the inside of her thighs as she slid her legs up and around his waist. He imagined that she'd smell like heady flowers.

He pressed his forehead to the glass with anguish. His cock was hard and throbbed for release. Giving in, he unzipped and unbuttoned the pants, letting them fall into a silky pool at his feet. He hissed as his hand slid over the turgid flesh, thumb sliding up and over the slit where semen had already beaded.

He was a man who, despite the elegant veneer, had dark and rough edges. He handled his cock with a sure and firm hand as he slid up his chest with the other hand and gave his nipples a hard pinch, imagining it was Lee's sharp white teeth biting him there.

He pulled up and off his cock, over and over, adding the second hand to take over after the first, stretching and stroking up and off, again and again, all the while thinking of Lee's sweet creamy pussy, her tight, sweet ass, those lips and that tongue. He imagined what she'd sound like, whimpering and begging him to let her come. The cool of the glass of the window at his forehead kept him moored in a small slice of reality, otherwise, he'd sunk into Lee, into her body, her sweetness, her sex.

He came with a hoarse cry of her name and shuddered as the fantasy slid away and he was left standing, alone, in his living room.

* * * * *

Lee's entire family had turned out to help and they had moved the entire contents of both apartments by nine. Aidan was amazed by the warmth and closeness they all shared and he felt touched that they had included him in their family.

His king-size bed went into the house's master suite and they affixed the light-blocking shades and the drapes to the windows.

"You know, as this is a four-poster bed, you could attach a frame to it pretty easily and drape the entire bed. That would make it extra safe," Em said thoughtfully.

"Yes, that would work nicely, so that even if the door to the hall was opened and light came in, it wouldn't harm Aidan," Lee said.

Each one of them had a studio. Lee's faced the afternoon sun while Aidan's was on the shaded side of the house. Lee's bed went into a guest bedroom along with an extra dresser. The house was so big that they didn't have nearly enough furniture to fill every room, so the family donated some and she'd shop for the rest as time went by.

Georgie came over with tons of food and they all ate at the giant dining room table that *tante* Elise had had in storage.

Her father raised his glass. "To my daughter and new son-in-law! Blessings and safety to you both. Love and longevity. Light and power and hope."

They all cheered and drank to each other and everyone filed out at eleven-thirty, dog-tired.

Aidan smiled at Lee. "I like your family a lot."

"They are wonderful, aren't they? And now you're one of us too. Although I would very much like to meet your grandmother and parents. Do you have any siblings?"

"My mother was only able to have me. But I do have people I consider to be siblings. Young vampires who lived with my family to be fostered. Three of them. One was born but her parents were killed, the other two were changed as children and needed a place to live and be raised. A sister and two brothers, but we're all scattered about the world. We all go back to my family's home for the major holidays, which include my mother's birthday," he said, laughing.

"Major holidays? Like Christmas and stuff, or do you have your own?"

"Both. We have a winter holiday, which is December twentieth, so we spend about two weeks at the family home in Ireland to celebrate it and Christmas. My mother's birthday is February seventeenth. We have a spring holiday, similar to solstice, in March and we all meet up there again for a few weeks each summer. They'll all love you. My sister is mated but my two brothers are still single," Aidan explained.

"Are all mates human?"

"No. It's pretty unusual, really. Most of the time they are other vampires, either made or born. In those rare occasions when we mate with humans, they are almost always witches or others with some form of gift or talent although I do know a few who were just accountants or secretaries." He laughed.

"Do most of them convert? To vampirism I mean."

"Yes. Most mates don't want to be apart. Some have lived normal human lifespans but it's very difficult on both people." He pulled her into his arms. "I know I couldn't imagine only having forty or fifty years with you."

His eyes moved down the line of her body and fixed on the fluttering pulse at the base of her neck as he spoke, and felt his cock come to life. "Now, I'm hungry," he said in a sexy growl, his incisors lengthening.

"Let's christen our bedroom, then." Laughing, Lee pulled away and ran up the stairs, tossing her clothing back at him as she went.

Once they got into the bedroom he pushed her against the door and pulled her clothes off. She tongued his ear while yanking at the front of his tee shirt, only letting go long enough to pull it over his head. She kissed down his neck while unzipping his jeans and shoving them down, freeing his rock-hard cock.

She murmured her satisfaction and knelt before him, gently scoring the backs of his thighs with her nails, leaning in to inhale the musky scent of his sex.

"Please, beloved," he whispered hoarsely.

"Please what?" she teased, flicking her tongue along his slit to gather the pearl that had seeped out.

He jerked at the contact. "Please suck my cock."

She took him into her mouth until his meaty crown tapped the back of her throat. He groaned and his hands flexed in her hair. She loved the way he felt, gliding between her lips, his skin silky and hard. She reveled in how she could make him whimper and tremble as she flicked her tongue under the head and nibbled gently, at how he gasped when she dipped the tip of her tongue into his weeping slit. He tasted so damned good, earthy and salty. She rolled his balls in her palm and pressed the pads of her fingers along his perineum.

He began to pump his hips, fucking her mouth, his hands gripped tightly in her hair. "Oh god, you feel so good, so hot and wet," he ground out. "I'm going to come, darlin'."

"Mmmm hmmm," she hummed and increased her speed, tightening her lips. He stiffened and his head flew back, he shouted her name hoarsely and shot his seed down her throat.

"God I love you," he said, pulling her up and grabbing her lips with his. "That never gets old, you know. I'm nearly two hundred and fifty years old and that was the best blowjob I've ever had. I definitely am keeping you."

She laughed and he threw her back onto the bed and dove after her. He widened her thighs and knelt between them, folding her knees back to open her up to him. He parted her with his thumbs moved down to taste her, sliding his tongue from the pretty rosette of her anus up to her clit. She sighed and ran her fingers through his hair.

She arched into his face and he stabbed his tongue into her gate, flicking it and gathering her creamy honey greedily. He moved up and licked and nibbled on her folds, two fingers stroking into her pussy, curved to stroke over her sweet spot, while his tongue sought the swollen bundle of her clit. She groaned his name and he sucked it into his mouth, causing liquid fire to course in her veins and trickle out of her pussy. With a lubed finger, he stroked over her rosette and slowly pushed a finger inside of her anus. She tensed and made a questioning sound but her clit continued to harden and she was gushing cream so he knew it was working for her. When he pinched her perineum with the thumb in her pussy and the index finger in her ass, she screamed out as her body bowed off the bed, wave after wave of pleasure coursing through her as she came.

He turned her over quickly and slid into her from behind, her pussy still contracting from her orgasm. Her inner muscles clutched at him as she thrust her ass back, meeting him as he pressed inside of her. He pulled her up so that her back was pressed to his chest, her bottom resting on his haunches. He cupped her breasts in his hands, palming the pert nipples. She laid her head to the side, exposing herself for his bite and he growled low and struck. She wailed out, coming, her juices flooding over her thighs and his cock. He pumped into her relentlessly as he drank from her neck, each swallow of her blood making him more intoxicated. Her moans and whimpers became more frantic as she bounced on his cock, riding him.

He tore into his wrist and held it out to her. She latched on and pleasure seared from his wrist straight to his balls. They pulled closer to his body as his orgasm gathered power, starting from his toes, barreling up his legs and into his cock until he exploded into her. He saw stars as he continued to be enveloped by her greedy pussy, as she continued to slam her body down on his, drawing out his pleasure until he was wrung out and they were both boneless.

He laid her down gently on the bed and she stretched against him, snuggling back into his body until she got comfortable and dropped off to sleep.

Aidan smiled softly as he watched the rise and fall of Lee's chest as she slept. Her hair fanned out over the pillow, her hand beneath her head, fingers gently curled near her sweet lips. She was so strong, but at that moment so fragile and vulnerable. His heart swelled with protective love. He'd never let this Damian hurt her, ever.

* * * * *

He worked in his studio until he heard her get up and move about. The house was great. He felt utterly safe and at ease there, nurtured. His creative juices flowed like never before. He scrubbed his hands and went into their bathroom to join her in the shower before he went to sleep and she went to pick up Alex from the airport.

"Hi. Did you sleep well?" he asked, getting into the stall with her and pulling her body to his.

She tried to think enough to answer but his fingers were busy. She had to close her eyes and take a deep breath when he slid a middle finger in a circle around her clit. As always, the moment she saw him or thought of him she was wet.

"I did. I don't think I've slept that peacefully in years. Did you get any work done?" she asked, ending on a gasp as he slid inside of her and nicked her neck, feeding gently. Since their mating, he only had to take a sip or two of her rich blood to be sated. Her back bowed as her climax hit, eyelids fluttering.

He didn't offer her his wrist right away, content to make slow love to her as the warm water soothed over them both. Finally, as his peak approached, he timed it and offered her his wrist and as always, the moment her lips touched his skin, tongue drawing his blood into her mouth, his orgasm shot through him like electricity.

With a sated sigh, he turned her around and kissed her lips gently. "This house is like heaven. You being here, our mating, I don't know if I have ever been this happy."

She smiled softly at him. "I didn't think that this kind of happiness even existed, Aidan."

He got out with her and dried off her and then himself as he went into their bedroom and watched her get dressed. "Are you going to bring Alex right back here?"

"I think I'm going to, yes. I want to talk with him about this whole thing. *Maman* and *tante* Elise want to meet him but that can wait. He and I need to get to know each other. We need to work out just what it is he's supposed to do, how he fits in with you and me."

He sighed and she cocked her head, sensing that something was bothering him. "What is it, love?"

"It's nothing, this whole thing is just wearing on me, I suppose. I'm worried for you and about you. This Alex situation, well, I feel a bit unsteady about what it's going to turn into."

"Turn into?"

"I'm jealous, all right?" He pushed a hand abruptly through his hair. "Having you dream about another man is just odd, especially when I know him and he's dreaming of you too."

She grabbed the hand that was in his hair and brought it to her lips. "Aidan, I love you. Period. I don't know what is going to happen or how this triad will work but you do know that I'd never do anything to betray you, right?"

He did. If he knew nothing else in the world, he knew that Lee was his woman and that she'd never go behind his back with anyone else. He also knew that Alex could never betray him.

"Thank you for saying it. I do know it, of course, but it never hurts to hear again." He gave her a sexy smile and kissed her on the tip of her nose. "All right, love. I'll see you when I wake up. Let's have a nice dinner tonight to welcome Alex to town, okay?"

"Okay."

She tucked him into bed and kissed him. After making sure the blinds and draperies were in place, she turned and left the house quietly for the shop. She'd leave for the airport later in the afternoon.

Chapter Six

Alex Carter felt as though the air had been sucked from his lungs when he caught sight of Lee waiting near the baggage carousel. He could see her aura clearly, a brilliant blue and white light surrounding her. She was strong and beautiful and he realized with a twist of his guts that he wanted her even more now that she was standing before him.

She turned and they locked eyes. The charge between them crackled with electricity. She gave him a slow smile and walked toward him. "Alex?"

"Yes. You must be Lee. It's wonderful to meet you. I've known Aidan for fifteen years and I've never heard him as happy as he's been in the last week. Every time I spoke to him on the phone all he was able to do was talk about you."

Lee felt the tug of his attraction and hesitated a moment. Alex noted it and sighed inwardly, this was his best friend's woman, damn it, he had to suck it up and deal. He reached out and hugged her hello, as she'd started to do right after he stopped speaking and the warmth of desire stole over both of them. The electricity of their mutual attraction singed his nerve endings, and it must have affected her as well because they both gasped and stood back, trying to pretend that nothing had happened and failing.

"Uh, okay. Well, let's get your luggage and get back to the house. We can have some lunch and talk this whole thing over until Aidan wakes," she said nervously, pulse pounding madly.

"Yeah," he mumbled. He held his carryon discreetly over his crotch to hide the erection that threatened to burst through the zipper of his pants.

They grabbed his suitcase and she led him out to the parking garage and drove him back to the house.

"So, tell me what's going on," he said as they entered the house and then stopped, turning around and taking the place in with awe. "Oh my god, this place, it's like a fortress. I've never felt warding this strong before," he said, wandering off topic as he set his bags down and headed into the heart of the house. "They're foundational, aren't they? I can feel layers of them."

She nodded. "Yes. They're in the dirt under the house and in the yard, the foundation, the wood, the walls, the wallpaper and the paint. You can see them in the tiles and the stained glass, even the wood flooring. They're worked into the banisters and the molding, too."

He faced her, awe still on his face. "This house is an oasis. I feel more at ease than I've felt in at least twenty years."

"Totally safe, I know. It's a relief really, once you walk into the door it's like a vacation from anxiety and danger." She led him into the kitchen. "Are you hungry? We have loads of leftovers in the fridge from a little celebration dinner we had last night. We've also got sweet tea, lemonade, soda and juice, as well as water."

He watched her delectable ass sway as she looked into the fridge. God, he wanted to be inside of her, hands caressing those creamy globes while he pumped his cock into her tight hole. He wanted to grab those curls in his fist and fuck her mouth. His desire for her was making him shake. He tried to look away but he couldn't. She slowly turned and they locked eyes.

"Oh my," she whispered. "What are we going to do about this?"

He shoved a hand through his hair roughly. "Nothing."

She laughed and the sound of it beat at his senses. "Alex, you don't think Aidan will feel this…this thing between us?"

"Aidan is my closest friend, I've known him for fifteen years. I'd get back on that plane right now rather than hurt him. I'd never betray him."

She put two plates on the butcher block table and pulled out the leftovers. She poured out two glasses of tea and motioned for him to sit down opposite her and began to eat. She thought of a way to say what she was thinking though she wasn't sure she understood it herself. "First of all, I didn't ask you to, nor do I want you to betray Aidan. Attraction is just attraction, it doesn't mean we have to act on it." She chewed on her bottom lip. "Alex, whatever is going on here, you're a part of it. You've been in my dreams, I've been in yours. You are integral to the situation. I know that much." She ate and thought for several minutes and he found himself becoming even more ensorcelled by her as he watched her process her way through the situation, concentration clear on her face.

Pushing her desire for him out of her mind she forged ahead. "Back to the subject at hand. There's a dark mage here, my mother and great-aunt believe him to be a death wielder. He sent his cadaverous minion to approach me for a meeting, to broker the terms of our surrender if you can believe that." She snorted. "He's set his sights on me. My mother, who is also a witch dreamer, believes he's out to corrupt my power and have me rule at his side. He's sent several magical attacks my way but thankfully things have all been okay and I've prevailed."

Alex got up and began to pace. "Damn it, a death wielder? That's some powerful shit. Why is he here? Why focus on you?"

"So I hear. Before I get to that, I have some questions of my own. Alex, what kind of magic do you possess?" She felt something dark about him, just at the edges, there had once been a taint there, now mostly gone but she didn't know that such things could ever truly be washed away.

"I'm a wizard, I was born into it. All of the men in my family are wizards."

"Yeah, I understand that wizardry is patrilineal the way the power in my family is matrilineal. I've, uh, well, forgive me my bluntness but I sense that you haven't always been on the path of light?"

He looked up at her, green eyes locked with violet and she felt the shock of their connection course through her body. "I am now. But I've held with dark mages in the past, Lee. It was a low period in my life and I'm not proud of it, but I wonder if that knowledge, my experience might be a reason I'm a part of this."

"You practiced the dark path?"

"Yes, for many years. My uncle and one of my brothers as well as my grandfather are all followers of the dark arts. My father is on the white path, as are my other uncles and brothers. I like to tell myself that it was youthful rebellion but it really doesn't matter at this point why I did it. What matters is that I did some very unpleasant things with my power and I have a responsibility to set the balance again." He sat back down and looked at her again, unable not to. "In my waking dreams, it's as if I am completing a circuit. Aidan is always there too, a part of it. Did I answer your questions thoroughly enough? Can you tell me what the hell is going on now?"

"My *grandmere* and *tante* Elise seem to believe that we are a triad, that the combination of you, me and Aidan is the key to defeating this death wielder. As to why he's here, why he's focused on me—well, it's a long story." She told him about the Compact and Damian Cole's wanting her power to help him break it and leave both the Charvez women and the innocents in New Orleans open to his dark magic and power.

"Wow. For what it's worth, I think I agree with your grandmother and aunt, if my waking dreams are right, the three of us are meant to deal with this dark mage." He shook his head to clear it and took a bite of his food. "Well, perhaps we should do a bit of work together then, to see what we can see. This house is the perfect platform for it."

"I assume that you and I have very different ways of accessing our power so perhaps we can work on piggybacking each other. Perhaps I can walk and you can project yourself out with me, be my backup?"

"Let's work on walking for a bit and we can go from there. My power is greater in the late evening, when the world is quieter. We should do it then, with Aidan as backup for both of us. First though, I want to get used to how your magic feels. Practice a bit, save the real walking for later."

He was afraid of what he wanted, of what he felt for her. He might have gotten rid of the taint of dark magic but what he craved from a woman was still dark and rough around the edges. He looked at Lee and saw all of the things he wanted to do to her, with her, it brought him to the point of madness because it tore at the loyalty he felt for Aidan. He'd just have to hold out until he could get back to Chicago and that was all there was to it.

Lee felt confused and panicked. The first moment she'd clapped eyes on Alex her pulse had sped up, her nipples had hardened and her pussy had softened and flooded. What she felt wasn't the depth of connection, of love and companionship, she felt with Aidan but there was a connection there nonetheless. She couldn't hide from her very intense attraction to him, it was more than just sex but sex was a major part of it. She felt Alex's lust beating at her and she wasn't even empathic. She was concerned for Aidan. She knew he'd feel it the moment he walked into the room with them.

She stood up, for the moment, pushing this thing between her and Alex out of her mind. "Are you tired? Would you like to rest for a while then before we start?"

"No, I slept on the plane. Do you have a place where you normally practice?"

"Let's go through to the library, I've unpacked it and have set up a ritual space. The light is really good, I think it may have been where magic was practiced before, it just feels like the perfect place for it. My supplies are in there already. Do you need anything?"

He shook his head as he grabbed his carryon and followed her. "I brought what I need." His eyes took in everything. The house was peaceful, and it already had her imprint. The hallway to the library had high windows and the light from them shafted onto the deep blue runner covering the hardwood floor. He saw boxes stacked in several rooms.

"Here we are. I did a basic blessing of the space last night with my mother and great-aunt."

He could feel it as he walked through the opened doorway. The room was large and had floor-to-ceiling windows with built-in window seats, the other walls were covered with large, built-in bookshelves that he could see were already partially filled with magical tomes and some novels. A large desk was off to one side and an overstuffed couch with two matching chairs sat near the windows. The room was furnished in a masculine way but the feel of it was feminine. He guessed it was the echo of her magic.

She kicked off her shoes and pulled the drapes across the lower windows, leaving the upper four feet or so uncovered so the room still felt light and airy. She moved about the room gracefully, lighting a brazier that she filled with sweet-smelling herbs. He watched the sensuality of her lips moving as she invoked the goddess to protect them as they worked, her hands drawing sigils in the air.

She motioned to a large area rug that was patterned with vines and berries. He toed off his shoes and stepped onto it with his kit. He felt the magic radiate from it.

"This rug is amazing," he murmured as she came toward him with a tray filled with different small items.

She gave him a beatific smile. "Thank you, my great-great-grandmother made it, it's been in my parents' home for years. My mother gave it to me as a housewarming present last night. A lot of magic has been practiced on this rug."

"I can tell." He pulled out his blades, the athame for pointing the way and the cutting blade to bring the blood. She looked at the sharpened blade and her eyes widened.

"I recognize the athame, but why do you have a sharpened blade?"

"Blood magic is very old, Lee. In and of itself, it is neither good nor bad, it's the intent of the user that determines that. I use the athame to point the way, the cutting blade is for the offering of a small bit of life.

"My magic is a combination of things. Where your magic, witch magic, comes from your connection with the earth, wizard magic comes partially from the earth, partially from the elements and partially from spells that trade upon power. You gain power through experience and natural talent. To become a powerful wizard you need natural potential and time, either that or you use dark magic and steal the power.

"Blood is the essence of life, I offer a bit of that in exchange for my power."

She nodded. "All right. Show me more."

He pulled the stopper from a glass bottle and washed his hands in ritual oil. Kneeling to the four corners, he laid out the blades, side by side and spoke a spell of protection.

The room began to hum with magic. The potent combination of male and female, of earth and sky, of fire and water, of her earth magic and his spell-based magic was strong. He felt the threads of it binding them together.

"I'm going to draw a circle of protection now," she said, pulling a velvet bag from the tray. He moved in a bit and watched as she poured the silvery line of sand around them. When she closed it he felt the electricity of it over his skin, felt their mingled energies flowing around within that circle like a warm tide. The potential of what they could do together hung around them like a haze.

She knelt before him, laying aside the bag of sand, her hands palm up on her thighs, waiting for him.

He removed his shirt and her eyes walked up the flat and muscular abdomen and wide chest where the amulet that his father had given to him when he'd come back to the path of light lay.

He picked up the cutting blade and, in a language older than the Latin she'd used in her spell, invoked his power and offered his lifeblood in exchange. "I'm going to offer my life and then, to tie our magics together, trace some runes on my chest and yours—most likely you'll recognize them. For this, I'll need your blood too. Do you offer your lifeblood freely?"

Lee nodded, her attraction to him nearly overwhelming now. Performing this kind of magic was so incredibly intimate that it seemed like foreplay. To share and mingle power with him was like him showing her his soul. Despite the fact that she knew she wasn't precisely cheating on Aidan, it felt like a very close thing. She had no idea how she'd be able to walk away from the man across from her. The intensity of connection that built from sharing this with him was frightening and confusing.

"Too bad Aidan isn't here, that healing saliva of his is good to have around," Alex joked and she laughed, some of the tension broken. He took the blade and sliced his palm until the blood welled up. She held out her own hand and he took it and cut her in the same place. Drawing the tip of his finger over the wound, he collected his own blood and reached toward her. She closed her eyes against the sensation of his touch, the magic sparking against her flesh. Her breath hitched. He drew the runes and pulled back but his pupils were wide and his skin was flushed.

"My turn?"

He nodded and she looked down at her forearm where he'd traced the runes and he was right, she recognized the symbols of binding and of combination. She collected her blood and started toward his arm but he shook his head. "No, here." He pointed to his chest above his heart and she traced the matching runes with a shaking hand. The energy and power of the markings shot through her and caused her to jump back like she'd been scalded.

Electricity crackled between them and he felt part of her take root inside of him. He knew she must have felt something similar by the way she looked at him, her lips parted, her eyes so expressive. He loved sharing this with her, he could feel how powerful she was, how powerful *they* were as a unit. It was so alluring and he knew that if it weren't for the intense connection he had with Aidan, he would have stolen this woman without a single guilty thought. But she was Aidan's woman and he had to find a way to live with the connection they had and walk away when it was all over, cherishing whatever he could from the experience.

"Okay, Lee, let's see if I can piggyback with you. Project yourself outward and I'll try and follow."

She nodded and he felt it when she pulled her power up from the earth beneath the house, felt it rush into her body and through her, into his. He felt it when she dropped her shielding and loosed herself and whatever it was that moored her in her corporeal self.

He turned his vision inward and felt her leave the room and grabbed her energy, catching a magical ride. He poured his magic into hers and hers flowed back to him, forming a kind of magical circuit. He hitchhiked on her power, it almost felt like he was in her head, watching as she flew out over the Garden District, through the French Quarter and the Central Business District. Through her, he saw the dark spots, not just the petty dark magics worked for silly vengeance but of far more concern, the more foreboding shadows of the kind of magic that dark mages used to gather power. The shadows of power being stolen.

He felt the oily shadow first and tugged at her consciousness, pulling her back to him, to her body. She saw it and they pulled back toward the safety of the house and the anchoring strength of their physical bodies. The power knew her, desired her, but saw him and halted for a moment, examining him and his defenses. In that moment, Lee struck out and hurtled the shadow back. Alex felt the perusal of the death wielder like the scratch of a long nail down his spine. He shook off his dismay and continued to concentrate on their link until they were back in the house and safe.

She opened her eyes, looked at him and stood up. "He's outside, he can't get past the gates." She spoke the words and broke the circle and their combined magic spilled out and flooded the room like a warm caress.

"I can feel him, his frustration. He's very powerful and he wants you, Lee."

"More than you do, Alex?" Aidan growled from the doorway.

Surprised, they both turned and saw Aidan come into the room.

"Aidan," Alex said and Lee heard the anguish in his voice. She looked at Aidan and let the depth of her love for him show through but she knew he could see the energy, the chemistry between her and Alex as well. He relaxed a bit but continued to stalk into the room.

"I can feel it, you know, your lust for her, the movies playing in your head," Aidan said to his friend quietly. There was anguish in his voice as well, sorrow, anger, frustration, all of the things Lee was feeling as well. He reached out for Lee's hand and drew it to his mouth, kissing her knuckles.

"I can't deny it. I'm sorry. But you have to know I'd never betray you. I love you like a brother." Alex looked at Aidan, pleading for him to understand. He felt jealous and guilty and covetous of the depth of connection he saw in that simple touch between Lee and Aidan.

Aidan pulled Alex into an embrace and the two men tried to remember just how much they meant to each other as well as to the woman now between them. "I know. I love you, too. She's mine though, Alex, my mate, my wife."

"Don't you think I know that? I wish to god that it wasn't happening, more than you do even. If I could turn it off I would. I'll leave." Alex's misery showed on his face and Lee's heart broke to see it.

"No, you can't. Lee needs you, needs your power and I need you, too. God, I've missed you, Alex." Aidan heaved a sigh and scrubbed his hands over his face.

Lee watched them both. She could feel Aidan's distress and Alex's misery. She brought the hand that held hers to her lips and let it go, moving to the window to look out while the two friends studied each other.

"You feel it too, Lee," Aidan said quietly, coming to stand behind her. She leaned into him, breathing him in.

"Yes," she said with plenty of her own anguish. "A wanting, a desire, a connection. It's different than what I feel for you, but I do feel it. I'm sorry."

"Are you wanting out of our mate bond?"

She spun around and kissed his lips, pulling him to her tightly. She pulled back and looked into his eyes. "No! How could you even think that? I'm your wife, you're my husband, that will not change, Aidan. I love you so much that it is literally my entire universe."

He pulled her back to him with a growl, his hand tightening in her hair, and angled her so that he could claim her lips. She gave a sigh of pleasure as her hands slid up his chest and into his hair. He devoured her, nipping at her bottom lip, kissing and biting his way down her neck until he pushed the bodice of her dress down and struck, just over her heart.

She gave a startled cry of ecstasy as his bite brought her orgasm. All she could do was hold on, hold his head to her as she rode the waves of pleasure until she could get her breath back.

Looking up into her eyes and then at Alex over her shoulder, he laved the nicks and closed them.

He relaxed and smiled at her, a predatory gleam in his eyes that brought a sound of pleasure from deep inside of her. He gave a darkly sexual chuckle and kissed her lips gently. "I am so relieved to hear that." He looked back at Alex, who, after nearly coming as he listened to his best friend make the woman he loved come, was now putting his kit away, desperately trying not to want the depth of passion and emotion he'd just witnessed and failing miserably. "But he is a part of this. I can feel that."

"Yes. I am sure of it, as were my *grandmere* and *tante* Elise. He's the key, more than that…" She searched for the right words. "Like a conduit or the final piece of a puzzle. He fits."

"With you?"

She shook her head. "With us."

Alex looked up at them and the yearning was there, naked in his eyes.

Aidan held out a hand to his friend and Alex joined them near the window. "We will have to work through this. For everyone's sake. For my sake, because I can't lose either of you."

Chapter Seven

Lee left Alex and Aidan alone for a while to talk.

"What are we going to do here, Alex?" Aidan asked as he handed him a beer.

Alex sighed deeply. "I wish the fuck I knew. I want your woman, Aidan. I'm sorry but I can't lie to you. She's amazing, beautiful, powerful, everything you said and more. Sharing magic with her only made it worse." He pressed his fingertips into his temples.

Aidan saw the cut on his palm and made an annoyed sound. He took Alex's hand and laved his tongue over the wound. "You should have told me you needed my help," he said as he let go, feeling Alex's blood course through his veins.

"I was a little distracted by jonesing after your wife," Alex said ruefully and nodded toward his hand. "Thanks, she's got one too, you should look at it when you get the chance."

Aidan nodded.

"This thing out there, it's bad, Aidan. It wants her and I'm afraid that if we can't come to some kind of solution between the three of us, that it'll take her. If this guy can corrupt her magic, use her distraction or her angst to get inside, he can turn her. If he does, there's no getting her back. She'll be his."

"We've got to find a way then, don't we? Lee's sister Em is something of a magical scholar, we should call her and get her looking into this situation between the three of us. I can't help but feel that with the dreams you two have shared, and the fact that you and I are connected, that this is meant to be and quite possibly the key to helping Lee defeat this threat."

Lee stood in the doorway, hesitating for a moment, not wanting to interrupt the moment between the two friends but both men looked up at her with hungry eyes.

"Darlin', can you contact your sister and have her look into this whole thing? The triad, the combination of witch, wizard and vampire—it just seems too coincidental to not look into."

Lee nodded. "Good idea, I'll call her now," she said and left the room quickly.

She discussed the situation in detail with her sister.

"Duh. I've been researching this since you and Aidan met that creepy guy sent by Cole." Em made a sound of frustrated annoyance.

"You have? Oh, well, that's good."

"You know, this is my job, my gift. It's totally common sense for me to look into it. I haven't found much but I did just locate some really old texts that I had just started translating earlier today. They have promise. I'll call you when I have answers."

"Are you mad at me?" Lee asked, not needing to be an empath to hear the agitation in her normally sweet sister's voice.

"No." Em sighed. "I just get a bit tired of people underestimating me."

"I didn't underestimate you! When we thought of it I came straight to you."

"Why not realize that I'd be on it? I know you're the powerful one, but I have a gift too, people seem to forget that." Another long sigh. "Never mind, I'm just being melancholy. Ignore me. I'll call you soon."

Lee let it go for the moment but resolved to have some one-on-one time with her sister, she was concerned to hear Em so down. "Okay, I'll be here. I love you."

"Love you too," Em said and hung up.

* * * * *

Later, Lee's mother and *tante* Elise came over and her mother's sharp eyes caught the tension immediately. She bussed Aidan on the cheek and placed a basket on the counter in the kitchen.

"Georgie is nervous, she's making feasts. There's enough food in here for the next week," she said with a wink at Lee. "You must be Alex." She gave him the once-over. "I am Marie Charvez, Lee's momma."

Alex took her hand and kissed it. "It is a pleasure, Ms. Charvez, to meet not only Lee's mother, but a very powerful witch." He turned and bowed to *tante* Elise. "And you must be the *tante* Elise that Lee has spoken of. I'm Alex Carter." He kissed her hand as well and Lee hid a grin as *tante* Elise gave him a flirtatious look.

"I felt you two this afternoon," *tante* Elise said as she sat down at the table.

"We saw the death wielder. He yearns for Lee," Alex said simply. "He is strong, his magic is very powerful. He let us go. Lee caught him by surprise, she's very powerful in her own right and I was also feeding her my power. But this Damian, he's got the taint of a demon lord on him."

Everyone shuddered.

"I was going to suggest that you dream walk, *cher*, and have Alex piggyback with you as backup. Now I don't think so. Hold off for a while, until we can figure out more about what is happening. Your sister is working on research, she's holed up in our library with her laptop and is snapping at anyone who disturbs her.

"In the meantime, you and Alex should work together, build some better defenses and, Lee, you need to keep working on your training. You know you're vulnerable when you are walking," her mother reminded her.

Tante Elise brushed her fingers along Alex's arm and stilled. "You walked the dark path," she said.

"Yes, I did. For six years."

"Ahh. You are here because of that. You are on the path of light, you have to let go of that guilt you carry. You made a youthful mistake, you have made amends."

He blinked at her, surprised at her ability to see right through him.

"Spooky, huh?" Lee said and kissed her great-aunt's cheek. She looked at Alex. "She's always pulling something like that out of her hat, you never know what she'll say next. Wait until you meet my *grandmere*."

Tante Elise gave a satisfied smile and then got serious. "What I'll say is that this Damian Cole is dripping with the blood and pain of his victims. That the souls he steals, the pain and misery he causes and trades to the demon lord he is tied to, have made him so powerful that he's only on the periphery of your grandmother's vision. We must find a way to defeat him, the sooner the better, because if he's more powerful than we are now, what will he be like in a month? I cringe to think about what the nameless, the homeless and the unwanted are facing out there right now. We can only protect so many and when one such as he needs power, they are the first to suffer."

"Or if he manages to grab Lee?" Lee's mother said, looking pale.

The five of them continued on for another few hours. Em came over later with some notes and they worked through dinner, brainstorming on how to approach the situation. After they left, Lee stayed in the hallway, watching and listening as Alex and Aidan talked. Sitting at the dining room table they had an easy back and forth clearly born of a deep bond. Their rhythm was easy, they finished sentences the other would start, picking up thoughts and ideas from the other. It made her feel even more desire for Alex. That he shared this level of connection to Aidan — she ended up feeling even worse.

"I am not a magic practitioner myself but I do know that there are old magics that are more powerful than any spells that you and Lee or Damian can wield alone. Death magics, and we know that Damian is using them, blood magics like the ones you two used this afternoon and sexual magics," Aidan said.

"That's not a bad place to look. My family has computerized a lot of the old texts. I think I'll give Em a call and get online and look into some of that. See if we can't find a way to use a bit of that ancient stuff," Alex said, standing and stretching.

"I am earth. My power is old and inherent. It contains aspects of all of those things, of birth and death, of blood, of sex. They are all part of the continuum — creation and destruction, winter and spring, maid, mother and crone. Pleasure, pain, procreation. Blood as life and death," Lee said as she came into the room and Aidan pulled her into his lap.

"That's giving me some ideas, Lee. I'll look around and see what I find. There are old texts of blood magics where they mixed with earth and fertility magics. Perhaps they can be used as an effective counter to Damian's death magic." Alex jogged out of the room to go and grab his laptop.

Aidan spun her on his lap so that she was facing him, sitting astride him. "You're so fucking beautiful," he growled, his possessive instincts blazing.

"T-thanks," she stuttered out as he pushed her skirt up her legs and grasped her hips, pulling her over his erection.

From his place on the curved stair, Alex watched the two of them as they loved each other, and felt such envy.

A pounding at the front door made them all halt and move into the entry. He and Alex moved Lee back. "We don't know who it is, stay back and I'll get it," Aidan said in a growl.

When he opened the door they all relaxed as the gray-haired ball of energy that was Lee's *grandmere* came inside.

"Gran, you scared us to death! We thought you were Damian!" Lee hugged her grandmother, who scoffed at the suggestion that Damian would just come knocking at their door, and introduced Alex.

Grandmere stared at Alex and nodded her head. She looked to Lee. "It's him and you know what you need to do," she said.

"What? Him what? You're confusing me," Lee said.

"Listen here, baby girl. You are the strongest and smartest of the bunch, yeah? I love you something fierce because you always do the right thing. This Alex, he's here for a reason, just as your gorgeous Aidan is here for a reason. The three of you, you form a triad. You need to make it a real triad in every way.

"It may not be easy to accept but it is what you need to do. I saw it clearly. You are earth, Lee, you ground the circuit, yeah? Aidan, he is life, blood. Alex, his magic makes him the sky, he is life through sex."

Lee blushed but Aidan nodded, resignation at the corners of his mouth. "We were just speaking of this. Of the old magics."

"You are old and wise, Aidan. You know what has to be done." She grabbed his hands and looked up into his eyes. "She is yours in a way that can never be unbound. What you and she share, it is given freely and this binding of the three will not change that. She has given her heart to you, Aidan. But the heart is capable of loving much more than we think it can. She will share herself, yes, but what she's given you is between you and her alone. That is between the two of you, always. If you cannot do this, if you cannot look within yourself and embrace this situation that fate has blessed you with, I do not know if she will survive. I cannot see her getting through this without her heart safely kept by you and him."

Things shifted into place and his resolve strengthened. He nodded and kissed her forehead. "Thank you, *grandmere*, I am honored that you would trust me with the heart and soul of your granddaughter. I understand what we need to do."

Alex came forward, placing his hand on Aidan's arm. "As do I. We will have to find a way. I love them both."

"That's how it will be then," *grandmere* said and marched back to the door.

"Wait a minute!" Lee exclaimed and caught up to her. "What the heck is going on? Are you talking about what I think you're talking about?"

Grandmere smiled at her and patted her cheek. "Ask them. I have to go or I'll miss Letterman."

"Well, let me drive you home then," Lee said.

"Oh no, don't worry, Rafe is waiting for me in the car."

"Rafe? Rafe the guy who works at the bakery?"

"Yes, honey, that's the one. I may be old but I'm not dead," she said with a laugh and a wave and was off.

Lee turned to look at the men and they broke off speaking. She was suddenly warily aware of their calculating gazes.

"So, explain. Just exactly what was she talking about?" Lee asked Aidan, her hands on her hips.

"Beloved, let's go upstairs and talk a bit," he said softly and held out his hand to her. She narrowed her eyes at that but took the hand he offered. He looked at Alex. "Why don't you get online and on the phone with Em to see what you can find about possible rituals? I'll call you in a bit, after I've spoken to Lee."

Alex nodded and grabbed Aidan's free hand. "Are you sure about this?"

"It has to be. You know this as well as I. We'll work this through," he said with a smile and led a confused Lee up to their room, shutting the door behind them.

"You are so beautiful. I've missed you today," he said softly and brushed his lips across hers. She softened in his arms and opened her mouth to him. He started gently, a brush of lips, a gentle caress of tongue, and got more heated. Before she knew it, he was plundering her mouth, devouring her until she was breathless. His hands were cupping the cheeks of her ass, kneading, his hips were churning, arching into her, his erect cock stroking over her mound. Her hands went to the waist of his pants and tore at them, trying to shove them down.

He broke off and held her hands. "Wait. We have to talk," he said, panting, pupils wide with desire.

"Talk? Are you joking?" she gasped out, trying to caress him. "You teased me down in the dining room and now you want to talk? I want you, Aidan. I've wanted you since two minutes after you took me this morning."

He smiled and pushed her down into the chaise and sat next to her. "It's good to hear that. I want you too, I never stop wanting you." He tucked a curl behind her ear. "But we need to talk. About you and I, about Alex."

She put her fingers over his lips. "I told you that despite whatever is between me and Alex, it's not what you and I have. More importantly, I'd never act on it. I love you, Aidan. I'd never betray you that way. And unless I am gauging him all wrong, he wouldn't either."

Aidan kissed her fingers and brought them away from his lips. "But we have to act on it. That's what your *grandmere* was talking about."

"What? What on earth are *you* talking about?"

"Beloved, we are each a part of the puzzle. The three of us have a part to play in this, as a unit and individually. You know that. You and Alex have dreamed of each other, you and I dreamed of each other. The three of us are meant to be together. Earlier tonight we talked about the old magics. Magics that combine different but very essential and powerful elements—sex, a very powerful way of creating power, blood, the essence of life, and earth, foundational power.

"You, Lee, you are earth. Even better, your magic contains elements of the other two as well. Part of your power is fecund, fertile, life, this is connected with blood and also, obviously with sex. My power is blood, I need blood to live but I'm a conduit as well between your magic and Alex's magic, a bridge. Alex's magic is sex. You can feel that, it's why the two of you are so intensely drawn together. His magic comes from the universe but more from out there." He gestured around the room and toward the sky. "Yours is grounded, his is mystical, mine is elemental. Triad.

"We need to join the three elements together to protect you. This Damian can attack you and defeat you on more levels than just magic against magic. He can insinuate himself into you and corrupt your magic, take it over and in that way, take you. If he does that successfully, you'll make him the most powerful mage around and we'll have lost you. This is what your *grandmere* was talking about downstairs. The ritual that we need to do will bind the three of us with blood and sex and your magic. When we do this, we, that is you and I *and* Alex, will be bound more than just temporarily. When you're bound to us, you'll be safer from Damian's attacks."

She gaped at him. "How? How is this going to make me safer?"

"It's just a hunch right now, based on some things I know and have read about that bubbled to the surface when we talked with your mother and Em, and also when Alex and I discussed things with your *grandmere*. Living for a few hundred years is pretty helpful that way. Alex is online right now researching it but this is what I think—if we bind you to us, you'll be ours. In that way, in order to corrupt your magic, Damian would have to take mine and Alex's too."

It made sense. Growing up in her family, she understood the delicate balance of her gifts. She knew that there were forces in the universe that were neither good nor bad but that were very powerful and that it was about who harnessed them and how. From Alex earlier, she saw that blood magic wasn't black magic and she got that sex and blood and earth could be a very powerful combination, used for good. *If* it worked. But still, it seemed like a heap of complication. "Let me get this straight, you want me to have sex with you and Alex? At the same time?"

He sighed. "It's complicated. On one level, who wants to share their woman with another man? On the other hand, it's not only necessary but fated to be." He shrugged. "I've felt unease about this since the first time Alex told me he'd dreamed of you. When I first walked into the room earlier today I felt his desire for you like a tangible thing. I felt yours too, like an undercurrent. It was a blow, I freely admit that. But then you looked at me I saw the love in your eyes and the pain eased, I saw the distress in

Alex's face, the anguish in his eyes. He was torn between his love of me and his love and desire for you. And he loves you, Lee. I've known Alex a long time and he's a very intense man, very isolated. What he feels for you, I can see it, feel it. It's love. How can I fault him for that? How can I fault him for feeling what I did when I first saw you?"

"Don't fault him then, but why on earth do you think we have to have a threesome?" She knew why but at the same time, she didn't know how to navigate her churning emotions — desire, angst, fear, anticipation.

He laughed ruefully. "Don't protest too much, Lee, I can smell your desire, I can hear your pulse speed up when you mention it, when I mentioned it. Yes, it does comfort me that it's not the same as when you are in my arms or even when you look at me, but it's there, is it not?" He stood up and began to pace.

"It has to be done. This Damian works in old magics, there's nothing more elemental than using death to gain power. You can't defeat that with your power because, despite how strong you are, you are only just coming into it. You need a ritual which harnesses those old magics in two ways. The first binds you to us, protecting you from Damian's attempts to corrupt your magic, and the second enables you to harness the power that we invoke for you. Your potential is there, this will give you another very strong tool to draw upon when you face him. The binding of my power, Alex's and yours will do that. It's meant to be. The more I thought about it today, the more I've come to believe it."

"This will ruin our relationship. Aidan, I'm really concerned that the jealousy would tear us apart. That I'd lose you and you'd lose Alex. It's too much to ask."

He knelt before her. "Oh love, you are my heart. Your *grandmere* was right, what you and I have, it's always going to be separate from anything you'll share with Alex. I have your heart, I know that, as you have mine. If I'm honest about it, I am a bit curious about how it will play out. If it was anyone other than Alex I don't think I could do it, for the future of this city or not. But he and I are really close and he loves us both. The bond will be of three instead of just two, this is more than just a threesome, Lee. What you and I have through our bond, it will be like that, only with three people. He'll be a part of us as you and I are a part of each other. We'll have to adjust to make it work but I think we can."

"There is no way I'd share you with another woman, ever," she said vehemently.

"Good!" He chuckled. "I don't want any other woman. I am yours, Lee. Forever."

"But will I be sharing you with another man?" she asked, more than a little turned on by the idea.

He got a small smile and shrugged. "We'll see. I won't close the door on anything."

Well! She got a shiver at the very lovely image that put in her brain. "Well, aren't you assuming a lot? That Alex will go along with this? I mean, what happens after we deal with Damian?"

"That will be up to him. He can be a stockbroker here and live with us, or he can go back to Chicago. I don't know what the bond will feel like, but if it's like what you and I have, I can't imagine that he'd want to be away from it." He shrugged. "Why don't I call him in and ask? Take a shower so he and I can talk and hopefully, we can begin to work this out."

She nodded and went into the adjoining bathroom.

* * * * *

Alex worked online for two hours, wondering what was going on between Aidan and Lee in the room down the hall. He'd found what he thought he was looking for in an old tome on binding rituals. The spell would work to bind their elemental powers together, as well as the three of them. As Aidan and Lee spoke the words that bound them together the ritual would not only bind the three of them together as one, but allow each to join as a bridge to the other with Lee's power as the conduit, the grounding element. He was fairly sure that this would shield her from being taken by anyone else and that it would make her stronger. He hoped so. The idea of losing her to the darkness ate away at him.

He heard their door open up and Aidan call out for him. Sighing, he closed his laptop and grabbed his notes, trying to steel himself for rejection but hoping for acceptance.

* * * * *

Alex came into the master suite and Lee's scent hit him like a fist. He moved his eyes around the room, taking it in, seeing bits and pieces of the life that she and Aidan were building together, her sketchbook on the low chaise by the doors to the terrace, a blouse tossed over the arm. There were a few boxes against the back wall. They were creating something there and he craved it. He met Aidan's gaze and caught the myriad of feelings there. Calculation, jealousy, love, brotherhood and if he wasn't wrong, attraction, too. He'd have to mull that one over.

"Well?"

Aidan shrugged and motioned to the chaise while he sat down on the bed. He explained the conversation and laid out Lee's concerns and Alex explained the ritual that he and Em had found and what he thought the results would be.

Primitive joy burst through Alex's defenses as he learned that Lee had been concerned about his feelings and that the plan was to go forward. "You're a lucky man, Aidan."

"I am. And so are you. This ritual, it will bind you to us, are you ready for that?"

Alex paused, finding the words. "You know what my family is like. You and your grandmother are the closest thing I've had to a loving family in my entire life. To have a chance at what you and Lee have... I can't put into words how seductive it all is. Yes, I'm ready to be bound to you and Lee."

"And you are ready to share a woman with another man? She'll never be one hundred percent yours, you know. She'll always be mine first, that's a fact. I'll have a part of her you can never touch."

"Aidan, I...you know me, you know that I have certain sexual needs. I've never met a woman who could ever match that, who I wasn't always holding myself back from. I'm forty-two years old and I've never been with a woman who made me feel whole, that I felt free to be myself with."

"And Lee makes you feel free to be who you are?" Aidan watched him intently.

"Yes. She's strong and I know what you and she have is different from what she and I will have. You're her mate but you know, deep down, she's mine too. That you are like my brother — " Alex shrugged, " — it will be harder in some ways but easier too, I suspect. I don't honestly know how I'll feel when this is over but I know we can work it out. Most importantly, we were meant to come together in this way, to strengthen her, to help her and protect her."

Aidan nodded. "I trust you, Alex, with my life, with my wife. If I didn't, you'd be dead right now for even looking at her the way you do." He held out his hand and Alex shook it.

"You're a better man than I am and I'm thankful for that."

Lee walked into the room in her robe. Her hair was still wet, skin flushed from the shower. A cloud of frangipani-scented steam followed her. "Is everything all right? Do you need more time?" she asked Aidan.

"It's all right, love," he said, standing. "We've talked it out. Are you ready for this?"

"As ready as I'll ever be. I don't know what to do. That is, how this can be a ritual and not just a scene from a wicked fantasy?"

Alex watched her, growing hard, heart pounding with the knowledge that soon she'd be his, that he would be theirs. He swallowed and found his voice. "I hopped online while you two were in here alone. I had the basic idea down but what I read and what Em found out filled in the gaps. The essence of the spell will bind us together as three into one. There is the physical aspect, as such, we'll need to join at the same time. Lee, you'll open yourself, be the conduit between Aidan and I. Aidan will take your blood first, then mine, while he's taking mine you'll take his and then mine. The climax will close the ritual as we speak the words. Lee, you know spellcraft, I'll let you word your part yourself. I've told Aidan what his part is. We'll all speak the spell at the end and hopefully it will work."

"Uh, okay. Join at the same time, huh?" She blushed but her heart was pounding, her nipples stabbing the front of her silky robe.

Aidan laughed and pulled his shirt off. "I think we can work that out."

Lee flicked her wrist and the candles lit. Alex hit the lights. He stood back and watched Aidan push Lee's robe from her shoulders and it fell to the floor in a whisper of silk. She was beautiful beyond what he'd been imagining, creamy skin, high pert breasts, the thatch of curls at the junction of her thighs—auburn like the hair on her head, sweet rounded thighs, strong calves and tiny feet. She helped Aidan out of his pants and he kicked them aside, pulling her to him, kissing her with leisurely passion.

Alex wasn't sure how to enter the scene. He watched the two of them and could feel the bond they had made together. He felt like an outsider and his loneliness welled up inside of him. The warmth and intimacy they had drew him in and his desire to have it, to share it, bloomed through him.

He pulled off his shirt and yoga pants and approached them. He reached out and ran his hands along the perfect curve of Lee's back and over the globes of her ass. She arched into him and he kissed down her spine, licking the small of her back and taking a bite of each cheek of her bottom. "So perfect," he murmured.

Lee pushed Aidan down onto the bed. She smiled down at him and he up at her, her hands caressing over his flesh, over the muscles of his chest and stomach, down the curve of his thighs and calves and back up, stopping to caress his balls and up over his cock. She ran her pinky finger over the head, swirling through the pearly pre-cum, and put the finger to her lips, sucking it inside. Both men groaned at the sight.

She turned to Alex and looked at his body and he felt caught in her gaze. He wasn't as tall as Aidan, he stood at just under six feet, but was broader, more muscular. His hair was as black as a raven's wing and was short and professional-looking but for the recalcitrant lock that perpetually fell down over his forehead. His eyes were leafy green and lazy, lips full but holding a hardness that Aidan's didn't have. His features were rough. Where Aidan looked like an angelic poet, Alex looked like a bricklayer or a bouncer. He touched her in ways that Aidan didn't, called out to the darker, deeper recesses of her soul. Where sex with Aidan was luxurious and beautiful, she had the feeling that it would be much more rough-and-tumble with Alex. It was as if each man fit into her soul in a complementary way.

She saw Alex's hesitation in crossing the boundary that she and Aidan had already created and could feel Aidan's comfort with what was happening but also his excitement at seeing her with another man. She reached out to Alex and put her hand to his neck, pulling him down to kiss her lips. When they made contact the electricity of it sparked through the room.

Alex growled low in his throat and pulled her tight against him. He nipped at her bottom lip, sucking it into his mouth, and swept his tongue into the warm cavern of her mouth, grinding against her teeth, caressing her palate and the inside of her cheeks, sucking on her tongue. She gave a mewl of pleasure and his hands came around her body, nails scoring over her ribs, and cupped her breasts. She broke the kiss on a gasp.

"Watch me touch you," he said in a low voice.

She looked down and watched his hands cup and knead her breasts. She arched into him with a surprised cry when he first rolled and then pinched her nipples. He lowered his head and took one into his mouth, swirling his tongue around the taut peak and then biting it. "Oh god, yes," she breathed out, the pleasure-pain rippling through her.

Aidan moved up behind her, pushed her hair out of the way and nibbled on her neck. She reached up with one hand and pulled him to her lips, delighting when she felt that his incisors had lengthened. She licked across them gently and he churned against her, his cock sliding up against her ass and the small of her back.

She had one hand gripping Alex's hair while he sucked and bit her nipples, the other had snaked back and encircled Aidan's cock. Alex dropped to his knees, kissing down her chest and stomach, his hands smoothing up her thighs and parting her to his gaze.

He smiled, seeing the glistening pink folds. "You're wet and ready for me," he said and she shivered and nodded. Aidan's hands had replaced Alex's mouth on her nipples and she arched into him.

"She always is," Aidan murmured as he watched Alex kneeling before her.

He looked up at Aidan and a slow smile slid over his face. "Good. I'm going to taste your honey," Alex rumbled and leaned in to slither his tongue along her slit, slurping up her juices. She groaned from deep inside and Alex looked up at her, commanding her to watch him with his eyes as he lapped at her. "So good and sweet," he murmured. He moved her thigh up onto his shoulder and she leaned back on Aidan, who took her weight easily and continued his torturous and sensual pumping of his cock through her fist as he kissed and nuzzled her ears and neck, palming and then pulling on her nipples.

Alex worked two fingers inside of her while he flicked his tongue over her clit and through her folds. He added a third finger and substituted the other hand to work her pussy, using the hand glistening with her cream to slowly tease over the rosette of her rear passage. She stiffened at first but then relaxed as he continued to eat her.

Alex slowly worked a finger into her up to the first knuckle. "Easy, baby, I'm just going to work you here, to stretch you a bit for my cock." She whimpered, at first at the burning from the intrusion and then in pleasure as he worked in another finger and began to scissor them, all the while fucking her with his fingers in both holes and lapping at her clit. The enormity of it—the all-out assault on her senses at having Aidan behind her, his cock in her fist, pearly wetness over her hand and back, his hands on her nipples, tongue in her ear while another man went down on her—she felt as if she were drowning in sensation.

She felt the orgasm approach. The beginning of a tingling in her scalp, goose bumps rising and heading toward her pussy from every part of her, nipples now impossibly hard and elongated, a pretty flush darkening her skin. Her breath was coming in short pants as she groaned over and over. It was one of those mammoth orgasms that you can feel approaching for what seems like hours, one that makes your teeth numb, where you scream out until you can't anymore.

And scream she did, loud and long as Alex latched onto her clit, sucking hard while pumping his fingers into her. Her legs lost feeling and without the support of each man, she would have fallen to the floor. She closed her eyes as the pleasure washed over her in wave after wave, wiping out everything but the twitching of her muscles, the pulsing of her pussy and the feel of the two men surrounding her.

She heard Aidan chuckle, followed by Alex, and felt herself being laid on the bed. She lazily opened up her eyes and saw both men give each other the smug, superior smile males do so well and then they looked down at her. She opened herself up and could feel no tension at all between the two men and was relieved. No matter how good it felt to be with both of them, she desperately wanted to avoid doing anything to hurt Aidan or their bond, which she could still feel strongly, wrapped around her heart and his.

"Wow," she said with a smile, slightly slurring her words and both men laughed. She reached out a hand to each and caressed velvet-covered steel.

"No, darlin', I'm already on the edge and we all need to climax at once for the ritual," Aidan said, gently removing her hand and kissing her fingers.

"I want to save it for when I'm buried deep in your sweet tight ass," Alex added.

"Are you ready?" Aidan asked her and it was her turn to laugh.

"Ready as I'll ever be." She sat up. "I take it that both of you will be inside of me at once. How do we do this, logistically?"

"Well, I've not ever done it but let me try this." Aidan sat up, back against the headboard. "Straddle me and put me inside of you and then Alex can come from behind and work his way into you. That way the feeding can be done easily, too."

Lee kissed him as she climbed astride him and slowly sank down on his cock, feeling him slice through her swollen wetness like a hot knife through butter. They both gave a sigh of pleasure and he leaned forward and nipped at her bottom lip. "I love you."

"I love you, too," she said, looking deeply into his eyes, fingers threaded through his hair, massaging his scalp.

She felt the bed dip and a wall of heat at her back as Alex moved into place. "I'm going to go as slow as I can, baby," Alex growled into her ear. "You're so tight and hot, I'm guessing you've never had a cock in here."

"No. Only fingers once or twice," she said, voice trembling with apprehension and excitement.

She heard a splat and then felt warmed lube slide down the crack of her ass. "I'm right here, baby, trust me," Alex said, working the lube in with his fingers. Moments later, she felt the head of him stroke over her rosette and she gave a shaky inhalation "Easy, Lee, I'm going to go slow. Press down as I push in, try and relax."

"Darlin', open yourself, be the bridge between the three of us. Relax and work on that," Aidan said around his incisors. She could feel his cock pulsing inside her, his hands at her waist. He gave her gentle kisses along her collarbone and moved his hands to gently cup her breasts. Alex put one steady hand at her hip, his fingers over Aidan's, and guided himself into her with the other one.

She threw down her barriers and reached out for Aidan first, felt his golden, warm touch and energy and established the link with him. She could feel Alex slowly pushing inside of her, could feel how stuffed she felt. There was burning pressure but soon bright threads of pleasure replaced the pain. She reached for Alex's energy and found it, cool and smooth like the sky at midnight, full of bright stars. He surrendered himself to her and through her, to Aidan. He then grasped out for her and Aidan and wrapped himself about them, threading his own link through theirs.

"Dear god, that's good," Alex whispered in awe. "I'm almost there, baby, just a bit more."

"Good, because I am so ready to come it isn't funny," Aidan quipped and they laughed.

Alex groaned deep and she felt his balls tap her flesh—he was all the way inside now. "Am I hurting you?" he asked, his voice husky in her ear.

"Fuck me, for god's sake, please," she whimpered, dancing the knife edge of another climax.

"You got it, Red," Alex said and pulled out and then pressed back in slowly.

Aidan waited through a few of Alex's strokes and worked a counter rhythm. She could feel each man shiver halfway in or out. "You can feel each other, can't you?" she whispered and got a grunt or groan in the affirmative from each. She dove back into the link and felt their pleasure as well as her own.

"I have to taste you, beloved," Aidan murmured around his incisors. "Alex, be ready, I don't think I'll last too long after I take Lee's blood and she takes mine."

Alex brought his wrist up to her shoulder so it would be easy for her to take from him and she watched as Aidan opened his own wrist in preparation. He struck her neck and she cried out, white stars of pleasure dancing across her vision, the honeyed ooze of her climax beginning to roll over her. She felt his pleasure through the link and he pulled her mouth to his wrist and then opened Alex's. She held both wrists to her mouth as Aidan fed from Alex, pulling her close to get to him. She felt Alex's surprised pleasure and then his triumph through the link.

Aidan was losing his battle to hold back his orgasm and shouted out in ecstasy as Alex took his other wrist and they both took from him while the two men thrust into her over and over. Alex leaned down and latched onto her neck where Aidan had struck, his tongue lapping at her and pulling her essence into him.

She felt golden warmth bolt through the link as her own peak continued to pulse over and over. A thousand threads wove the three of them together, the room was humid with magic and sex, sweat and blood. Lee was wedged between both men as they pumped in and out of her, loosing their seed inside. She couldn't move but was buffeted by their pleasure and her own. Her head rested on Aidan's shoulder as she whimpered out the last edge of her climax.

"Now, Lee, speak your part now," Alex gasped.

"As we will it so it shall be, we three are one as the one is three. So mote it be," she whispered and made a protective sigil in the air.

The air in the room was shimmering like heat from the pavement.

Alex held up his wrist, still bloody, and joined it with hers and Aidan's, their blood trickling down wrists and arms, mixing, the blood of three becoming the blood of one. He was speaking in another language, a spell of protection and also of unleashing. A humming began and he and Aidan spoke the last lines together.

Lee felt wave upon wave of energy buffet her, she was suddenly standing, no, floating, arms out as both men looked up at her. She could feel her veins fill with power, her cells fill with the magic that was born of her own uniting with theirs. It was something unique and special. It felt as if she knew it all, felt it all. She was powerful in a way she'd never imagined. She felt the heart and soul of both men residing inside of her like brilliant stars.

She rode on the joy of the moment for a bit more and then instinctively reined it back in and ended up kneeling on the bed between them again, the room still twitching with magic but no longer brimming over with it.

She looked at both of them and began to laugh. She saw Alex smile, genuinely smile and laugh in response and Aidan hugged both of them and they all collapsed back onto the bed.

"I think it worked," Aidan said.

"Oh, I know it did. It's almost too much, the power is rushing through me like the ocean," she said lazily. "We're really going to have to change these sheets."

They looked at her and then down at the mess on the bed and laughed. "Oh, baby, I like that you can think of such practical things at a time like this," Alex sighed and kissed her temple.

* * * * *

She awoke some time later and got up, making sure the windows were properly covered and the doors locked. Aidan found her in the kitchen, drinking a glass of orange juice. She'd lost quite a bit of blood earlier and needed to recharge a bit. He smiled as he saw her taking care of herself, smelled the sweetness of the burning herbs and leaned down to kiss her shoulder and put his arms around her waist.

"Are you all right?"

"Yes. I should feel exhausted but there is so much stuff running through my mind right now, I feel like I've slept for a week." She turned to him and stood on her toes to kiss him. "Are *you* all right?"

He sighed and sat down, pulling her into his lap. "Yes, I'm more than all right, actually." He stopped for a moment, thinking over his words. "You see, before last night, I thought that I could do it because it was what needed to be done to protect you, to make you the strongest you could be against Damian. I would do anything to protect you, even share you." He smiled at her and she smoothed a hand through his hair.

"But now, I can feel his link too, I can feel *our* link. It's right, it's meant to be and I can't argue with that. I don't resent it, I'm not jealous of it. Alex is now as much a part of our bond as you are." He shrugged. "It may not be Ward and June Cleaver, but it's what we should be. Watching you with him, it was beautiful."

She hugged him tightly. "I love you so much, Aidan. You're my heart. I'm so glad it's okay, I've been worried. It's so clear that you two love each other and to have ruined that, I never would have forgiven myself."

He shook his head. "You have nothing to feel guilt over. Now he means even more to me, before he was the brother of my heart, now he's the brother of my soul as well. We share a great love and trust, Alex and I. And now we share something even more special, our love of you. More than that, I know you'll be safe during the day. If you need help and I can't get to you, he can."

"How are our families going to deal with this?"

He laughed. "Oh, who knows? Let's just take one step at a time, shall we? Defeat this dark mage and then we can deal with everything else."

"I'm too wired to sleep, I think I'm going to work for a while," she said, getting up and stretching.

"Good idea, I think that's what I need, too." He gave her a measuring look as he went up the stairs behind her. He reached out and grabbed her around the waist and carried her into her studio. "After I get some more of you," he said in a thick voice and she laughed until he set her down on his lap and his cock.

They both worked until the sun came up and he carried her into their room and they got back into bed. She smiled when she saw that Alex hadn't moved from the position he'd been in when she'd first gotten up. She snuggled into Aidan's back and sighed with pleasure when Alex woke up enough to move into her curve of her body.

Chapter Eight

"Little one."

Lee realized that her dream was being walked by another person. She tried to throw up a defensive shield around herself but the magic didn't work. She looked in the direction of the voice, which now was giving off beautiful laughter.

She blinked her eyes against the brightness. "Who are you and why are you walking my dreams?"

"I am Freya, although others have called me Cerridwen and Circe. I am a being of magic, of light and sorcery. I am here because the Compact I made with the one who came before you is in great danger of being broken."

Lee squinted against the magnificence of the woman before her. "I can't see you. Can you turn it down a bit?"

Again the melodious laughter sounded and then the light dimmed. Lee looked up and saw a beautiful woman with flowing white-blonde hair, wearing a striking necklace and a cape made of feathers.

"Is that better, Little One?" Freya asked with an amused smile.

"Yes, thank you. You say the Compact is in trouble? We had an idea that this dark mage might be here to destroy it but very little idea how."

"That's because he is here to destroy it. Do not underestimate Angra, he is a very old and powerful mage, he has been on Earth as long as I have. He has teamed with a demon lord, I will not say his name but he is the one I was in battle with, the one I forged the Compact with. Together they are nearly invincible and they will destroy your beautiful Crescent City — as well as all of the innocents in it — if the Compact fails. And, Little One, you know it won't end there. This darkness will spread outward."

"I don't understand. Yes, the Compact made the Charvez women protectors, but you must know that even without it we wouldn't just walk away. We would, of course, continue to protect those who needed it. It's the price for our gifts. We freely give that."

Freya smiled sadly. "It's more complicated and more bleak. If the Compact fails, you will all lose your power. There will be no more Charvez witches, not in the way you all exist now. Of course, it also bears saying that if the Compact fails, it will mean that Angra has gotten to you and corrupted your magic."

Lee felt the shock of the statements go through her. She'd sort of understood about her own power being taken over but the reality of the loss of the Charvez magic nearly floored her. "We would all lose our gifts? Even the generations to come?"

Freya nodded. "Yes. While the one who came before you had natural gifts, it is the Compact that gives you all your power. It is the conduit from me to your female line. If the Compact fails, that feed will die and so will your power. If Angra corrupts you, he will drain your power first and then strip the rest of you of it when he breaks the Compact. But I must tell you that you are the key to this. Because the Compact was drawn with a witch dreamer, you, the most powerful witch dreamer, must be the one to defend it. The other women in your line are strong, yes, but I foresee that it is you who must break Angra's power. You are the only one who can."

"Oh my god," she said softly, fear licking at her heart. The responsibility that she'd so blithely ignored for most of her life fell to her shoulders. "Just who is this Angra person, anyway? The dark mage said his name was Damian."

Freya tsked. "You know very well that a name gives power. He would not give his name of his own free will, so I will tell you." Freya hesitated, cocking her head as she looked Lee over.

A beatific smile broke over Freya's face. "You have joined, your power is threefold now."

"Uh, if by that you mean that I did a binding ritual with Aidan and Alex, yes, we did it earlier tonight."

"This is a good thing. You are much more powerful this way, their power flows through you and your inner core, your heart and soul, belongs to your two men. Little One, this just might save you, save the Compact. In this battle to come, it will be more than a straight measuring of power against power. Do not get complacent about that. Angra will use whatever he has to to win, to keep you off balance. I feel better about you now, about your chances of coming through this fight successfully."

"Can't you just help us? Step in and stop Angra, or make sure that if the Compact is broken, we don't lose our ability to protect innocents? It's not like we are using our powers to clean the house and work at the circus or anything."

Freya smiled softly. "I am bound by very few rules, Little One, but even one such as I has a few. I cannot interfere just as the demon lord cannot. All I can do is try and help you within the rules. I cannot just bestow power on mortals, it comes through once in a very great while that I am allowed to do so for something monumental, in the last instance, to you and yours through the Compact. But if it is lost, I cannot just give it back. I am sorry, I wish I could." Freya stopped speaking and looked about the immediate area, startled.

She turned back to Lee, speaking urgently, "I must go. This demon hunts in the realm of dreams and I do not wish to draw him to you. You are strong but not invincible. Protect yourself and those you love. I am sorry to say that you will face grief and sorrow ere the end of this." Freya approached Lee and touched cool lips to her forehead then, with a bright flash, was gone.

* * * * *

Lee came awake and saw that it was already ten-thirty and that Alex was already up. Leaning over and kissing Aidan, she got out of bed, hit the shower and wandered downstairs where she could hear the clicking of a keyboard and Alex's voice. She came into the living room and saw him, shirtless, laptop open, barking orders at someone. She stood in the doorway and watched him as he worked—the absolute concentration on his face, the speed with which his fingers moved over the keys—and smiled. So utterly different from Aidan and yet, he held her heart too.

As if she'd called out to him, he looked up and saw her there and a grin broke out over his face. He was like a completely different person when he smiled like that. "Okay, you got all of that right? Don't forget to call those clients about what I just told you. You know where I am if you need me, but don't call unless it's an emergency." He hung up the phone, signed off the computer and stood, stalking toward her.

"Good morning," she said, head cocked. She watched the sinuous, powerful way he moved with a bit of apprehension and a whole lot of anticipation.

"Good morning to you, baby," he said in that low throaty voice. "I've been waiting for you to wake up."

"I woke up and worked for a few hours last night, it was a good night. I finished a painting and started another. I must have been really inspired." She raised an eyebrow and fought a grin.

He reached out and pulled her to him, pulling the robe down until her hands were trapped and her naked torso exposed to his gaze. "Let me inspire you some more."

He ran his free hand up her body and pulled her lips to his. "God, I want you. I want you ten different ways and I don't think that will be enough."

She strained against his hold, arching into him to feel more of his skin against hers. "I want to touch you," she said, slightly breathless.

"You will, when I'm ready for you to." He kissed and nibbled his way along her jawline, down the column of her throat and to her nipples. He flicked the tip of his tongue over each coral-colored peak and she squirmed and made noises low in her throat. "I love your breasts. So perfect. High and pert."

"Small."

He bit her and she yelped. He laved his tongue over the sting. "Don't. Don't ever berate yourself, Lee. They're perfect. You have two men slobbering over them. How could Aidan and I be wrong?" He let go of her hands and the robe slid off. "Touch yourself, baby, see how perfect they are." He brought her hands up so that she could cup herself and pulled away, watching her.

And what a sight she made, bottom lip caught between her teeth, hands at first hesitant but growing bolder, her eyes going half-lidded as she ran her palms over her nipples. Nipples still wet from his mouth.

"Sit down on the couch," he said and she backed up a few steps and sat. He followed her and yanked the buttons on his jeans open. His cock sprang out and she sighed happily as she gazed at it. She reached out and caressed him, he was thick and hard.

"Suck me, Lee."

She looked up into his eyes, eyes that were so frequently shuttered. Now, though, it was as if the leafy green had deepened. His normally restrained manner was relaxed. She squirmed and squeezed her thighs together, his commands were making her hot and wet, her skin itchy. Still sitting, she leaned forward and slowly took him into her mouth and, with a swirling lick, looked up into his eyes.

He hissed. "That's it, make me wet. I'm going to fuck your mouth nice and slow and then I'm going to throw your sweet ass over the back of his couch and fuck you until you scream." He made a hum of appreciation as she moved closer, eyes on his cock, licking her lips.

She opened her lips and pulled him back inside her mouth, making him glistening wet with her saliva. His cock was red and shiny as it slowly pushed in and out of her, her lips gliding over him. She dragged her nails over his balls and then over the tight skin of his abdomen, delighting in how the muscles jumped at her touch.

He had her head between his hands, guiding her, controlling her speed. She licked along the edge of his crown and he groaned. "Yes, that's nice. A little bit of teeth, oh yeah, right there." She nibbled on the sweet spot beneath the crown and he shuddered.

He kept on, gliding between her lips, her tongue swirling and flicking, her teeth gently nibbling and he pulled out, panting. He bent over, pulling a condom out of his pants pocket. She took it and rolled it over him.

Grabbing her, he quickly moved her so that she was bending over the back of the couch, ass in the air, open to him. He moved behind her. "I can see how wet you are. Tell me what you want me to do," he ordered as he nudged her feet to open her legs wider.

"Please, I want you inside of me," she said, voice quavering.

He dropped to his knees and pressed his face into her pussy, devouring her, holding her wide with his big hands. Relentlessly pushing her higher and higher. He lapped at her, sucking on her clit, even gently pinching it between his teeth. She was sobbing with need, ramping up higher and higher. He drew the flat of his tongue over her rosette and warmth spread through her. He nibbled on the cheeks of her ass, his fingers plumping her clit while he licked and pressed his tongue inside of her. She squealed with surprised pleasure and then groaned hard when she began to come, drenching his hand, arching up to give him more access to her, her hands fisted in the pillows of the couch. He stood up and slammed inside of her, hilting in one hard stroke and she screamed out.

"You taste so good, baby," he crooned as he pulled out slowly and slammed back inside of her. "You feel so good, your pussy clutching at me, creamy and soft. I wanted to fuck you long, hard and slow but I don't think I can now. Your lips drove me too high, the scent of your pussy, the taste of you on my lips, I need to come inside of you, and right now."

"Yes. Oh please. Hard and fast," she panted and he stroked a hand down her spine and set it at her hip to steady her as he drew in air and began to fuck her in earnest, just as she'd begged, hard and fast. He moved a hand to her clit and she tried to move it away. "I can't, it's too much."

He moved her hand and went back to her, drawing circles around her clit with the tip of a finger. "You can and you will," he said with a grunt. "Give me your hands."

She did, and he held them at the small of her back while he teased her clit with the free hand, occasionally dipping into the well of her pussy to keep her nice and wet. "Someday soon I'm going to tie you to that four-poster bed and have my way with you," he said, still slamming into her, the sounds of moist flesh meeting flesh echoing through the room.

She began to come again, shocked that it was still possible after the night before. Her inner muscles clutched at him as she whimpered and arched to meet his thrusts.

"Oh yeah, that's it. I'm coming." He groaned long and hard and slammed into her once, twice and three times more before he threw back his head and hoarsely cried out her name. She felt his cock jerk and spasm and they both slumped to the floor.

They lay there together, getting their breath back, enjoying the contact and the quiet. Alex was satisfied, so intensely satisfied that he almost didn't trust it. He'd never been with a woman and not held a part of himself back, the full nature of his sexuality wasn't anything he'd been able to unleash before. If he was rough it was usually with a partner he didn't have any real feelings for, if he had feelings for her, he was careful to hold his darker nature back. With Lee, he could let go and not fear the rebuke in her eyes, not fear feeling the intensity of adoration and love he had for her and could feel from her in return. It was a balm to so many inner wounds.

Lee turned and looked into his face. She traced his lips with the tip of her finger. He was so complicated. Aidan was pretty much open, he wasn't simple really, but his layers were something she understood. Alex had a lot of layers, she knew it would take time to understand what made him tick. He could be so intense and sexual one moment and then achingly tender the next. It was surprising and it kept her a bit off balance. She enjoyed seeing the different nuances of this man.

Some minutes later he nipped the finger tracing his lips and sighed, standing up. He reached down and helped her to her feet, embracing her.

"That was a very nice way to start the day." She winked and pulled her robe back on. "Okay, now let's work. I had a visitor in my dream this morning."

He gave her an annoyed look. "Why didn't you say so?"

"I wanted you to fuck me first. Now we can get down to magical work." She grinned at him.

He couldn't suppress a grin in return. "I seem to be freeing you inner slutty girl."

Lee gave a surprised laugh. "Thanks for that."

"My pleasure. Now, let me make you some lunch. I want you to be fueled up for the afternoon."

"We should go to my *grandmere*'s shop to meet my mother and great-aunt. We need to be there by one. I can't believe I haven't even asked you yet, but have you ever been to New Orleans before?"

"First, tell me about your dream. Are you all right? Was it the dark mage?" He reached out and took a corkscrew curl and twined it about a finger.

"Yes, I'm fine. I wouldn't have let you fuck me if I'd been injured, silly. It wasn't Cole, although his name is Angra and he's apparently very old. Freya, the angel-slash- goddess who made the Compact is the one who came to me. She told me a lot. But let's get going, I'll have to tell it all to my family anyway so let me tell a very long story once."

He sighed. "Fine. I'll wait. Now, to answer your earlier question, no, this is my first time here. Pretty stellar vacation if I do say so myself."

She gave him a crooked smile. "Then why don't we get some lunch in the French Quarter? Get some good food into you to fortify you to face the entire female side of my family."

He laughed. "Let me get dressed and shave. Want to get a shower with me?"

"That would only lead to more *inspiration* and we don't have time for it. *Maman* is not to be trifled with," she said with a smile and they headed up to get dressed and ready.

* * * * *

Lee parked her car near the shop and they walked to the Gumbo Shop for lunch. She ordered a variety of dishes that she thought he'd like and they enjoyed sweet tea.

"It's really wonderful here," he said, digging into his plate of stuffed redfish.

"I'm biased of course, growing up here, but I love it. Is it too different from Chicago?"

"Well, yeah, it's very different than Chicago. It's different from most places I've been. I know we've got a lot on our plates right now but after this whole thing with the death wielder is over, I hope I can see more of the city."

"So, uh, I know it's early and you might not know yet…" She hesitated and looked into his eyes, trying not to sway him with her own feelings.

He took her hand and kissed across her knuckles. "You don't ever have to mince words or hesitate with me. I don't think you can understand just how complete you've made me feel, I'm whole for the first time in my life. You did that. Talk to me."

"Are you going to stay here in New Orleans with us or go back to Chicago?" she asked quietly, watching him as she ate.

"What do *you* want me to do?"

"You're part of me, part of us. I want you here, forever," Lee said simply. "I know it's odd. Heck, two weeks ago I was a single girl with relatively few complications in her life and suddenly I met Aidan and we had this connection, we bound ourselves together and got married. You show up and throw the already topsy-turvy world even crazier and last night we bound ourselves to you and it feels like you've been in my heart and soul forever, just as it does with Aidan." She shrugged. "I know it's got to be hard to share with another man. I understand if you have to get away from it and have your own life and your own woman. I'd miss you, but I love you enough to let you go if that's what you need."

He was quiet for a moment as he studied her and then that beautiful Alex smile broke over his face, softening him. "I want to be here too. I can't imagine not being with you every day. I can't imagine not being with Aidan every day. It was hard enough before, when he moved here to find you. Now that we're bound, I don't want to imagine what my life would feel like without the two of you in it. I just needed to hear you say it."

After lunch, they walked over to the shop and went inside. Alex's eyes widened as they entered. The shop was not overly large but it was filled with magical items. The air sang with it all. It smelled sweet, like the herbs Lee had burned the afternoon before when they'd worked magic together. There were shelves filled with bottles and jars of herbs and tinctures, crystals hanging in the windows, casting brilliant prisms over unexpected places. As she guided him through the shop he stopped to look at the different cases and curio cabinets holding jewelry and figurines, candelabras and other magical ritual paraphernalia. There were shelves holding books from many different magical traditions.

The counter at the back, where the register was, appeared to have been made from a single piece of timber. The wood looked smooth and shiny, like it had been touched thousands of times. The magic that hung in the air was intensely feminine. "This place is incredible," he murmured to Lee.

She smiled, letting go of the breath she'd been holding. She'd been hoping he'd love it like she did. "It is, isn't it? I've been to a few other shops like it in other places but none seem to have everything this one does. Then again, my family has operated it for generations in one form or another so I'm probably not the one to give an unbiased assessment."

"Who've you got here?" Em asked as she walked out from the back rooms. She smiled when she saw that it was Alex.

Alex gave her a hug and a kiss on both cheeks. Lee watched her normally reserved sister open up to Alex in a way she didn't see very often. It made her heart glad to see not just Em accepting Alex in such a warm way, but seeing Alex's clear affection for her sister.

Em looked them both over. "It worked."

Alex grinned. "It did. Thank you so much for your help yesterday. So much research! We couldn't have done it without all of the translation work you did. You're amazing. My family has an extensive collection of magical books and documents, I'm sure that I could arrange for you to look them over sometime."

Em's eyes lit up at the prospect even as a blush worked over her face and neck at the compliment. "That would be wonderful, I'd love it. Thank you."

"We're family," Alex said and realized that he meant it.

Em smiled at him and then at her sister. "Lucky girl. You can't just be happy with Aidan, you have to have this one, too? No fair," she said and kissed Lee's cheeks.

"An embarrassment of riches," she murmured into Em's ear and they both laughed. Alex looked between the sisters uneasily. Em turned to him and clasped his hands between hers. "Don't worry, Alex. Welcome." She kissed his cheeks too and was gone with a wave.

Lee took his hand and led him into the back, where her mother and great-aunt were waiting.

He leaned in and kissed her quickly but oh-so gently and gave her a smile of such tenderness that it squeezed her heart.

Her mother stood up on a gasp as they entered the room. *Tante* Elise merely looked at her with a raised brow. "So strong. Your aura, Lee, *ma cherie*, you are so brilliant it blinds me."

Lee motioned for Alex to sit. She poured them some tea and explained about the ritual that they performed to bind themselves, skirting around the more graphic portions of the evening.

Her mother walked around her, looking carefully. "I think you can take him now. He will know that you are stronger, though. Anyone can see it, which means we should move quickly."

"We should walk his dreams tonight, catch him unaware," *tante* Elise said.

"Speaking of dream walking, I had a visitor in my dreams this morning. Freya, the being that made the Compact. She told me the secret name of power of our death wielder. He is Angra, and is apparently as old as she is and very powerful." She filled them in on the rest of the conversation, carefully recounting the bit about the Compact's failure meaning the loss of their power and the fact that she would have to be the one to defeat Angra because she was the key somehow.

Lee's mother's eyes widened at that. "Did she tell you how to stop them?"

"No. She couldn't." Lee explained about the rules binding Freya and her last comment about seeing sorrow before the end. She looked into the eyes of the people she loved so much. "If the Compact is broken, we lose everything." Which was an understatement.

Lee's mother put a hand to her throat in alarm. "Well, then we'll be sure not to let the Compact be broken."

Her *grandmere* came into the room and nodded at them. "It worked, I see. He can't take your power now, it belongs to Alex and Aidan. You belong to them. In order to corrupt you, he'd have to corrupt them first. He will be very angry about it and will kill you before he lets you win."

A shiver of fear worked up Lee's spine but she nodded. It had to be done, Angra had to be faced and vanquished. It was the only way to keep them all safe. "Let's work then," she said to her mother and *tante* Elise.

For the rest of the afternoon they worked spells, Alex sharing his spells with them and the Charvezes theirs with him. He helped show her how to keep her powers reined in and controlled and she was pleased by the results. She got to know him even more as she watched him handle his magic, watched how confident he was with his power, with his own magical tradition.

"I want you all to be safe, stay within the house or the shop. He's going to know soon that I have accessed my full powers and have Alex as my partner. He will strike and I don't want it to be at you," Lee said to her family.

"I've been dealing with bad guys since before you were born, girl. I hide from no one, this is my city," Elise said with her head held high.

"Of course you have, I mean no offense. I just want you to stay safe. We've all agreed that I'm the best person to do this. I'd be nowhere without you and *maman*," Lee said soothingly.

"Uh-huh. You just remember who taught you your tricks, girl," Elise said haughtily.

* * * * *

Angra plunged the knife deep into the flesh of the body before him and his eyes went to half-mast in pleasure as he spoke the ritual words and the essence of the dead slammed into his body, strengthening his power.

He kneeled before the stone altar and placed a goblet with the heart in it on top. He spoke a spell and called the demon lord, drawing the sigils in the air that would open the gate into the human dimension.

The stench of brimstone nearly caused Angra to gag, he'd never be used to it, no matter how many millennia he lived to smell it. The demon stepped out of the gate and into the room, taking the heart and tossing it into his maw casually.

Angra did not look at the demon directly, even a dark mage found it difficult to take in the horror of a demon lord as powerful as this one was. It spoke to him in a language older than recorded time and its voice was a horror to hear, it made Angra's flesh recoil, made him think of dark painful things.

"Angra, the she-bitch has contacted the witch. Why have you not taken her yet? I grow tired of this. Once the Compact is dissolved the immense well of power here can be mine."

"She is well-protected. I'm working on it. Her current dwelling is warded so powerfully I cannot even enter the gate surrounding it. I'm not concerned about the vampire, he cannot help her. She's strong but not strong enough to defeat me. I will take her and corrupt her, and then she will be mine. Do not forget your promise to me. I have served you faithfully for millennia, I want this witch to be my queen. Do not harm her."

The demon lord made an annoyed snarl accompanied by a cut of his hand, dismissive and derogatory. "I have no need to fuck female human flesh. I want her power, give me that and you can have her body. Do it soon or feel my wrath." With a quick movement, the demon lord jumped back through the gate and Angra quickly closed it, relieved, as always, that the demon lord was gone from this dimension.

* * * * *

After Lee and Alex left the shop, they walked back to the car quietly. The heat of the July afternoon was oppressive but there was something else lurking. "He's been here. I can feel it. I'm glad Simone and Em have moved in with my parents for a while," she murmured uneasily.

Alex was on guard as they drove back to the house and didn't relax until they got inside. He knew the feel of dark magic in the air, he'd practiced it enough. He felt secure enough in where he was today that he knew he could withstand it, but at the same time the temptation to take the dark path would always be a part of him. The worst part of it wasn't the presence of the darkness, but that for the first time in his life he had something he was afraid to lose.

He was sullen, thinking that while on one hand he'd gained something immeasurable with his bond to Lee and Aidan, he'd lost his biggest defense — the fact that he had nothing to lose. He was also worried that he and Aidan wouldn't be enough to save Lee.

"You're awfully quiet," Lee said as they stood in the kitchen, preparing dinner.

"I can feel the dark searching for you, wanting you."

"Why did you do it?"

"Turn to my grandfather's way?"

She nodded as she continued to slice up garlic and peppers. Aidan came in and kissed her gently, and surprising both Alex and Lee, dropped a quick kiss to Alex's lips as well before he hopped up to sit on the counter, watching them both.

Pushing any thoughts about the kiss to the back of his mind, Alex turned back to Lee's question. "My family is old and powerful. We've been a force to be reckoned with as dark wizards for generations. Oh, there were those who followed the white path, a few from each generation, but they were a subset, a minority, and certainly not powerful enough to change the direction of the family.

"Anyway, my father decided to break from his father when he was in his twenties and got married and had a family. He's a strong wizard, very powerful in his own right. We, my brothers and I, were raised apart from the rest of the family, and my uncle had taken the place of my father, who would have been the next leader of the family at my grandfather's death. We were classically trained by my father and one of his brothers and a cousin, all wizards who'd left to follow the path of light.

"Then my eldest brother came to me and asked me to come and meet the uncle who'd stayed with my grandfather. He was the oldest and next in line to lead after my grandfather passed. My brother had been meeting with him secretly and was ready to leave our family to go and live with them." Alex continued to chop vegetables without looking up, as if he'd gone to another place while recounting the story.

"I went out of curiosity, and they all used what my brother had told them to lure me. They used my vanity and my desire for power. Within the year, I'd left as he had and I became one of my uncle's strongest allies. My grandfather doted on us, we had the power, wealth and respect that we didn't have with my father.

"I sank deeper into it and it got into my pores, into my soul. With the path of light, you achieve things slowly because it is a sharing of power, an exchange and you learn as your power learns to trust and respect you. With the dark path, power comes quickly because you steal it, you take it from others, you make exchanges with less-than-honorable forces in the universe and what you exchange isn't something you've earned. Everything you touch is drained dry by your need to supply more, to get more power. It becomes an addiction, an obsession.

"I was twenty-seven years old when I heard a vampire nest had moved into Chicago. Now, to capture the essence of a vampire, especially an old one, to traffic that essence to the dark would have garnered me a lot of power. I could have surpassed my uncle, even my grandfather, with that. So I went and engaged in a relationship with one of them, saying I wanted to be a donor. She was beautiful and powerful and very old. I befriended her and earned her trust and then I killed her and took her power."

At this, Alex hung his head and sighed. He looked up at Aidan, who gave him a small smile of encouragement, and went on.

"On my way back to my grandfather's compound I was run off the road and knocked out before I could use any defensive magic. When I awoke I had been captured by Aidan and his grandmother's people. I was very weak, they'd drained me nearly to death. I don't know how long I lay there on the edge of death but it was long enough for me to have a serious look at what I'd become. I vowed that should I die then, I'd do it on the right path."

Lee thought about the kind of courage and character it took for someone to confront their own faults that way and accept them and truly want to make things right.

Aidan interrupted then. "He confessed what he'd done to Malia and why. He was truly remorseful and gave himself willingly in her place. My grandmother, who is a very wise woman, took to her rooms for a week to consider the answer and in the end she decided that we should let Alex go. We did and he went back to his mother and father, back to the path of light, and he's been there ever since. We kept contact and became friends and then like brothers. He's a very different person than he was the first time I saw him, he's come a very long way in fifteen years."

Lee reached over and kissed Alex gently. "That's some long winding road, Alex. I'm so amazed by you, so proud to know you."

He blushed a bit, surprised that he still could. "I'm still dark in many ways. You know that."

She snorted. "Why, because you were once?"

"No, because I can't see you without wanting to take you hard and rough, without wanting to make you beg. Because I love to fuck your sweet ass instead of just your pussy like a gentleman. Because I love to order you to suck me off and command you sexually. I'm not a nice man."

She cocked her head and sighed in exasperation. "So because you like to be dominant and a bit rough you're a bad guy? Oh, please. I've been with bad guys, okay, and you aren't one. If I told you to stop or if it looked like you were truly hurting me, you'd stop immediately, wouldn't you?"

"Of course!"

She looked at Aidan and rolled her eyes. He gave her a grin and a wink. She looked back to Alex. "Would you protect me from harm if you could?"

"Yes, you know that."

"Do you respect me and my wants, my beliefs and power? Do you believe me to be your equal?"

"Yes, yes, and yes." Alex began to see the point she was making and the beginnings of a sheepish smile broke over his face. He felt like every moment with Lee was healing him.

"So shut the fuck up already about being a bad guy. I *like* it hard and rough with you, if I didn't, you'd know it. Having you and Aidan...you're like the complementary parts of my soul, of my heart. What each of you brings to me makes me whole."

Alex blushed again and kissed her hard on the lips and would have done more but his cell phone started ringing and he groaned. "I'm expecting a call, I've got to get that. I'll be back."

She nodded and then turned to Aidan. "You hungry?" she asked, unbuttoning her shirt and easing it off.

He jumped off the counter and gave her a growl, nodding.

"Dinner is served," she said in a whisper, unzipping his jeans and reaching in to caress his throbbing cock.

He pushed her back until her torso rested on the island in the kitchen, then ripped her silky panties from her and shoved her skirt up, exposing her to his view. His eyes had bled to amber and his voice deepened and thickened as he murmured to her. His mouth went to her nipples as he combed his fingers through her wet heat.

"I'm ready for you. I need you inside of me, please," she said, looking up into his face.

He nodded and slid into her in one long delicious stroke. Her ankles clasped at the small of his back, her arms spread out, holding onto the counter. The dishes clanked together as he thrust into her slickness. He looked down, watching himself disappear into her and then pull back out, her juices making his skin red and shiny.

"You are everything," he said and she moaned as he began to slowly flick the tip of his finger over her clit in time with his thrusts.

"Yesssss," she said, trembling. "You make me feel so good, so right."

"I'm going to taste you now," he said around his incisors and leaned down, striking at her breast, just above her heart. She shivered and shuddered and moaned as his lips touched her, tongue teasing her blood out, hearing him swallow her. He just needed a small taste as the ritual last night had provided him with more than enough blood but he couldn't resist even the smallest bead of her blood.

The incredible rush of pleasure hit her and she bucked beneath him, hips arching to meet him as her pussy milked him, clutched at him, flooded with honey. He leaned down, forehead against hers, and came with a long groan of her name, slamming into her tight body over and over, cock throbbing as he emptied himself into her.

He continued to hold her there, head on her chest, both of them panting. She was so wrung out and it felt so good to be against him that she stayed that way for several minutes, only moving finally because her back was killing her.

"Feeding has never been so much fun," he said with a wink and helped her down. She moved to the stove and began to sauté the vegetables.

"It had better not have been," she said back with a wink of her own.

During dinner, she explained her dream visit to Aidan and they decided to go ahead with the dream walk. Aidan had spent several hours that evening conversing back and forth with Em, both of them researching Angra, and texts about demons weren't bedtime reading.

According to the ancient texts, Angra was the personification of evil and darkness. There were differing accounts but at one time at least, Angra was seen as a god who, due to some act on his part, had been cast out by other dark spirits to walk as a human in the human realm. He'd been a human for at least three thousand years and had been causing death and destruction alone and in concert with evil spirits and demons since before that.

They surmised that the demon lord had chosen him specifically to attempt to dissolve the Compact because his power for chaotic magic was very strong. He was able to unravel white magic.

One thing they knew for sure was that with each day he became stronger and that with the Compact in jeopardy they had to move as soon as possible. Aidan was worried for both of them but agreed to act as their ground for the dream walk. Even if Angra wasn't sleeping, Lee was pretty sure she'd learned enough from her mother and great-aunt to slip into his subconscious mind without him seeing.

After dinner they moved into the library and Alex laid out his kit while Lee made her own preparations. She lit the incense and spoke her spells of protection. Aidan sat back and watched them both, the fluid grace of his woman and the steadfast self-assuredness of his best friend. They complemented each other like bookends.

Lee noticed the change in her magical abilities and attributed it to the ritual. In the past when she'd performed rituals, she knew her magic was there by reaching out to feel it. Now the feeling of being enmeshed by protective magic was palpable and strong. Instead of calling magic to her, she merely activated the magic *within* her.

She drew the salt circle and the three of them sat inside. She turned to Aidan and grasped his hand. "You aren't a witch or wizard but you do have magical strength. Don't break the circle, but you can enter the walk with me and pull us out if need be."

Alex spoke a spell of protection and grasped hands with Aidan and Lee to complete the circle of three. He felt the power of it hum along his skin and he glanced at Lee who gave him an excited smile that he found himself returning in kind.

Lee opened herself up and felt both Aidan and Alex along the link. She drew them up and out, spiraling through the night. She could see, as she looked out across the magical plane, the dark miasma that signified Angra's presence. She headed toward it and into the center.

She navigated into his subconscious and walked it. He wasn't dreaming, he was awake and performing a ritual. He was using death magic and the stench of it hung in the air.

She stood there watching, figuring out where he was, who his people were, for some time, until he stopped what he was doing and thrust his consciousness inward, facing her.

"Such a brave act for such a weak little girl," he said, a snarl curving his beautiful lips. It was a pity really, Angra was a handsome man, long and lean, flowing black hair, regal nose and lips, beautiful brown eyes. Lee thought somewhat ridiculously, that evil men should all be ugly.

She sniffed, bored. "Uh-huh. Is that all you've got? If I'm so weak, big man, why do you want me so badly?"

He narrowed his eyes, she could feel the rage vibrating through him. She flicked her wrist and threw the hot yoke of his anger off.

"I want all of the women in your family. You'll be my dark queen of course, but the rest can be in my stable. I'll suck them all dry." He shrugged. "It's a side effect."

She laughed. "Where do you get this stuff? B movie scripts? Look, you had your chance to get out of New Orleans and you haven't taken it. This is your final warning. The Compact makes this city ours and we aren't giving it to you. Your testosterone levels are making you delusional enough to think you can take this city. You can't. If you aren't gone by morning I'll personally kick your ass."

Before he could answer she withdrew and was back in the library, the line between them snapping before he could reach back to her.

"Wow, you make me all hot and bothered when you act like a warrior goddess," Alex said with a grin.

"If you confront him in the morning, I can't help you," Aidan said seriously.

Lee gave Aidan a smug smile. "Oh, I lied. We're going to take him tonight. He's in a warehouse in the Central Business District. He's just done a killing ritual, with the blood of the innocent he's murdered, he'll be powerful but not powerful enough. I'm going out back to perform a ritual of my own. Aidan, do you need to feed from Alex? I want to be sure you haven't used too much energy going into this." Standing, Lee breathed the magic contained within the confines of the circle back into herself. Then, hand clasped with Alex's, she broke the circle. She felt incredibly powerful and aware, just the kind of mood to vanquish a dark mage older than Christ.

"I'm fine. Your blood was incredible before, now it's supercharged. I'll get changed and ready." Aidan gave her an admiring look, Alex was right, she was very sexy in warrior goddess mode.

"I'll come with you, babe, if you don't mind. I'd like to watch your ritual and do one of my own," Alex said and she nodded.

In the back, under the big willow trees, she shed her clothing and stood skyclad beneath the moon and stars.

"What kind of ritual are you going to do, love?" Alex asked, watching the fluid sensuality of her movements.

"I'm going to ask the goddess for power and protection, and make an offering." She knelt and touched her forehead to the earth and then, arms outstretched, she asked the goddess for forbearance, power, justice and wisdom. She called on the elements for protection and camouflage and using Alex's blade, sliced into her palm and let the blood drip onto the ground, making an offering. The air crackled with energy, the wind caressed her, the earth welcomed her blood sacrifice and she could feel nature, the goddess accepting her plea, taking in her offering, protecting her and hers.

Alex kissed her hand helped her into her robe. She sat on the ground and watched, fascinated as he made his own offering, speaking a spell in that odd language he used for his magic. The air around him crackled with energy and tiny arcs of light echoed around his hands. Each word he spoke, each movement he made seemed to create power that reverberated around him almost like a cloak. His magic was more theatre than hers was, more mysterious. It had an air of secrecy, of mysticism—a lot like the man himself.

Chapter Nine

Angra roared in frustration as the witch disappeared without a trace. His consciousness had surfaced after he tried and failed to follow her back through the link she'd traveled to him.

"What is it, master?" one of his faithful asked fearfully.

"It's that witch! She's been here, in my head." How dare she give him an ultimatum! She was nothing, a weak nature magic practitioner with a bunch of herbs, while he was the blood god of darkness.

He'd have the bitch. He'd corrupt her magic and make it his own and in doing so split the Compact asunder. From the demon lord, Angra knew that the Charvez witches would lose their power when the Compact broke. He had done his homework and found the spell to have in place to suck that power into himself. He'd protect Lee, making sure she kept her power as long as it was on his side. He'd sire countless children on her and start his own empire in this magical city.

He had been so angry when he was cast out and made human but over the last two thousand years had warmed to it. Not his exile, he hated that. But to being a human mage. Humans were flawed, he couldn't deny that, they had short lifespans, their bodies ached when injured and when they aged, but they felt in ways he never could when he was a god. In truth, he had the best of both worlds—his powers were still nearly invincible and as a man he could taste the delights of the flesh he could only partially feel as a god. Together with his queen they'd usher in a new era of darkness and their seat would be right there in New Orleans. Yes, they'd all bow to him in the end. And he had a plan to get that Charvez witch, *his* Charvez witch in line that very night.

* * * * *

They drove toward the Central Business District, Aidan at the wheel, Lee and Alex quietly conserving power.

"Park here on this block. We'll walk, it's only a few more blocks from here," she said quietly.

They got out, Aidan shifting into mist, Alex walking just behind Lee. They could feel the stain of Angra's magic in the air, it pressed at them as they got closer. Lee had her link to her mates open and signaled that the next building was the one they wanted. Aidan went ahead and took out the three men at the door, as silent as the mist whose shape he took.

Before she went inside, she and Alex wove a spell of protection around themselves, linking energies and magic. It felt like links of chain mail, fluid but strong. Aidan didn't need the same kind of protection, as he could shapeshift, but she sent him a bit of protection anyway and he gave her a crooked smile and blew her a kiss. An act at odds with the savage way he took one of the men down when they entered the warehouse.

She and Alex followed Aidan inside and came to a large room off the first floor. Angra was there with his henchmen and a hooded figure tied to a chair. He turned and saw her, a grin on his dangerously beautiful face.

"Oh, you don't disappoint at all. I knew that you'd be coming sooner or later, sooner is always good when it comes to winning."

"Stand down or I'll kill you and every one of your little friends, too," she said, her power simmering. Of course she was going to kill him no matter what, it had to end that way. If he left he'd only start trouble somewhere else. She took in the hostage but also the multitude of people in the room. If she made a grab for the hostage, she might lose Angra and that couldn't happen. He wasn't even particularly near the hostage at the moment. Once she vanquished him, she'd help the hostage. Her heart ached with the choice but it was the only one she had.

He watched her with a calculating glance. "If I didn't know better I'd think you tapped into the darkness to grab a bit more power for yourself. Not a problem, once your power is mine it'll be a good thing."

She yawned and sent out a bolt of energy, knocking two of the men on his right up and off their feet. They slumped to the ground.

Angra moved quickly to send a fireball her way but it bounced off the protective spell that she'd placed around them.

She let her power course through her, loosed the reins until it shimmered about her. Her feet left the ground and Alex stepped forward, chanting under his breath.

Angra stepped back and put his arm about the figure tied to the chair. "Parlor tricks. It's all you witches have. Come a little closer, why don't you? Let's see what you've got then."

She moved forward, trying not to think about the hostage in the chair. She had to deal with the other threats first, damn it, but she hated having to do a benefit cost analysis with someone's life and the stark truth was that one life wasn't worth more than the tens of thousands of lives that would be affected should Angra and the demon lord win. The bubble of energy surrounding the triad pushed everything out of their way. "Are you so sure you want to see everything, Angra?" she taunted, using his real name, his name of power that Freya had given her. That knowledge weakened him. He blinked out his shock.

"How did you find out?"

"Oh, a mutual acquaintance told me." Lee tossed a fireball at him but with a flick of his hand it hit the wall behind him. Alex wove an energy spell and it hit Angra's leg, eliciting a sharp curse from him. Angra kept his arm around the person in the chair and Lee forced herself to not think about it, she had to vanquish this mage no matter what.

Angra sneered at Alex. "What's this? A pet wizard? Oh, he'll be fun to put on the payroll too. I smell George Carter on you. You're a long way from home, aren't you, boy?"

Alex ignored him, continuing to feed his power into the spell he was working.

Lee dug deep, thrusting down and pulling power out of the earth below her feet. She struck out at Angra again, this time pushing her power into his body until his back bowed. Aidan had taken out the remaining men in the room and was leaning against the doorjamb, licking a drop of blood from his lip.

"Get out, bitch!" Angra roared. He grabbed his blade and stabbed it into the person on the chair before she could stop him. He began to speak a spell, draining the power from the dying figure. Lee could feel his power grow, she also felt a sharp pain in her chest.

"No," she whispered, moving closer, her concentration wavering.

Angra finished his spell and tore the hood back from his victim and Lee nearly lost consciousness.

"*Tante* Elise!" she screamed and Alex grabbed her wrist sharply, pulling her aside as he sent out a barrier to protect her from the spell Angra hurled at her. Tears ran down her face.

Concentrate! Lee, she's dead and he just drained her power. Damn it, you can't let go right now or it's all over! Alex screamed along the link. Aidan sent her his power, his warmth flowing through the link, reassuring her, steadying her.

Lee turned back to Angra and unleashed herself, the electricity she released made her hair stand on end. She felt her rage build along with her power, it was battering against her control, threatening to cause her power to whip out of her grip.

"Control it, Lee! It's getting loose. Darlin', hold on or it's all over," Alex ordered and she snapped back to herself and reined it in.

Angra began to call his demon lord and Alex countered, keeping the gate the demon would use to enter their dimension from becoming solid. Lee advanced on Angra then, fury roiling in her veins, her power crackling, bent on revenge, on removing him as a threat to anyone else.

"She tastes so good. What will you taste like?" Angra taunted.

She ignored his taunts, felt him probe her, trying to find a way into her power, to gain control but he couldn't and he roared with frustration. "What have you done?"

"I'm beyond you," she said solemnly and reached out to him. Once her hands made contact with him she spoke an unraveling spell to break his magic down. He struck at her and bloodied her lip but she ignored it, concentrating on the spell as he tried to fight her off and open the gate at the same time. She felt him begin to rally, fortified with Elise's stolen magic. His defensive magic cut bloody slashes into Lee's flesh, but she pushed on.

"Stop! We could be so good together, you can't do this! I'm a blood god! Rule at my side!" Angra screamed with anguish.

"You are nothing," she said coldly and suddenly, he was nothing at all. He was gone from the room and she slumped down, Aidan catching her, speaking softly, trying to reassure her.

She pushed him off and rushed to the chair where her great-aunt lay nearly dead. "*Tante* Elise, hold still, let me try and help." Lee reached deep inside for a spell to put her great-aunt back together again but *tante* Elise grabbed her wrist in a surprisingly strong grip.

"T-too late...let g-go. Watch yourself...n-not dead, gone," she croaked, losing more of her life as the seconds passed.

"You will not die!" Lee ordered and began to work a healing spell.

"Already dead...*ange*," *tante* Elise said softly and Lee felt a part of her own heart die as she felt her aunt's soul slip away from her body.

"No! Damn it, you can't let yourself die!" Lee screamed but Elise was gone, her body empty.

"I'll clean up the taint. Aidan, why don't you call Lee's family to come down and take care of Elise?" Alex said, caressing Lee's cheek for a moment and then moving back to use his magic to clean the area of the dark magic stain, the echoes still hanging in the air.

Aidan nodded and helped untie Elise's body while he called Lee's mother's cell phone. The women had already gathered at the shop, having felt both the battle and Elise's death. He hung up and looked down at Lee, who was rocking her great-aunt's body in her arms, using her last bit of strength to cleanse her of Angra's touch. He ached to grab her and clean up the bloody wounds all over her body but he knew that she had to expend her grief at least in part.

"She was always so loving, she understood me more than anyone else in my family ever did. I got her killed, it's my fault," Lee whispered.

"It's not your fault, it's Angra's fault and you know that. You tried to protect everyone, it doesn't always work out," Alex said as he sat down with them, exhausted from his own use of magic.

Lee's mother came rushing in the door with the other Charvez women right behind her, the men following in their wake. Her mother rushed to her and held her face in her hands. "You did it, *cher*. You beat him," she said softly.

"I didn't win, he took *tante* Elise's power, he killed her and I didn't stop him. She said he wasn't dead, that he'd escaped." Lee's voice was barely recognizable from her crying.

Lee's *grandmere* pulled Elise, her last living sister, into her arms as she sobbed.

Lee's father took the whole scene in, wishing he could spare them all the grief. He put his hand on Aidan's shoulder. "We should get out of here and soon. We'll have to figure out what to do with Elise after we leave. You can't explain this to the cops, not even in New Orleans."

Eric and Aidan helped Lee stand, her legs shaky from the grief and the drain on her power from the battle.

"Let me take her, you're both wiped out too," Lee's brother Eric said to them and took Lee up into his arms. She put her head on his shoulder and he sighed deeply and kissed the top of her head gently. "It's okay, short stuff, we're all gonna be okay."

Chapter Ten

That was the last thing Lee remembered until she woke up in her bed, Alex on one side, Aidan on the other, both men curled protectively around her body. The sun was up, she could feel it and she craned her neck to see the clock. It was nearly noon.

She got up carefully, her legs still unsteady, and headed for the shower. She cranked up the heat and stood under the water, wanting to wash the poison of the night before from her skin. She stood there for what felt like an hour, weeping, scrubbing at her skin until she heard someone get into the stall behind her.

Alex had felt her leave the bed and slowly surfaced, coming out of sleep. He heard her turn on the shower and gave her a few minutes, aching to hear the sobs but knowing that she needed to be alone at least for a little while. At last he could stand it no longer and he went into the bathroom.

His heart nearly broke when he saw her, head bowed and weeping, her hands furiously scrubbing. He could feel her grief through their bond and it washed through him, nearly sending him to his knees. He climbed into the shower and pulled her to him.

"Shhh. Oh baby, let me scrub your back," Alex said gently, taking the washcloth from her and softly rubbing circles into her back, her arms and legs. She stood there letting herself be dazed by the slow rhythm of his movements. He helped her out of the bathtub and dried her off, pulling her robe on and brushing her hair out.

"Let's go downstairs, your family said they'd be back here this afternoon. Your mother, Em and Eric all slept over."

She nodded and let him get her dressed and they walked downstairs, where she could smell the chicory coffee brewing and hear the hum of voices. Her mother, sensing Lee's presence, came out of the kitchen and pulled her into her arms. "Oh, sweet girl, you look so pale. Come into the kitchen, I've got some herbs brewing and your *grandmere* has some tea for you."

Lee allowed herself to be pulled into the room and sat down in a chair next to Eric, who put two waffles on a plate and slid them in front of her. She didn't want to eat but her *grandmere* gave her "the look" and she relented and made herself drink the tea and eat the food.

"What are we going to do with *tante* Elise's body? How are we going to explain it?" Lee asked after she'd finished eating.

"We've taken care of it. We wove a spell over the coroner, it wasn't hard. As far as he knows, she had a massive heart attack and was dead before we found her. They released the body to us directly. We'll have her funeral on Wednesday. Your daddy is handling the arrangements with your cousin and your uncle," her *grandmere* said, waving the scent of the herbs toward her. "How are you feeling? Did that tea help?"

"I'm fine. I'm the one alive," Lee said sarcastically.

Her *grandmere* walked to her and took her face between her hands. "No more of that. You stop it right now. Your auntie, she loved you but she also understood her power and her responsibility. You holders of the Compact, you have no easy road. Sure, some generations of witch dreamers pass without a hitch, and some don't. It's dangerous, as you very well know, as she knew. Her death wasn't your fault. The three of you did all you could."

Lee felt the breath hitch in her throat. "I could have made him free the hostage right away but I didn't. I saw the hooded figure tied up there but I didn't do anything about it. I should have known it was her."

Eric kneaded her shoulders and she felt Aidan stir at her distress, groggy, struggling against the power of midday and she sent reassurance back toward him, as did Alex. He sent love and dropped back into unconsciousness.

Alex took her hand and squeezed it in reassurance. "Lee, baby, you knew the situation. You had to take him out. The hostage, *tante* Elise, was next to him, it's not like you could have helped her. You had to deal with Angra first. You took out his lackeys, the ones Aidan didn't, anyway. You couldn't have known he'd lunge so fast at her. You had no way of knowing who it was." Alex continued, trying as hard as he could to reassure her. "I was there, you were holding him off, holding off his power and the attempts to tap into your own power. You had to focus on him."

She sat there, listening dully as they all sought to reassure her that she'd done everything she could.

"And it was all for nothing. He's not vanquished, he escaped," she said, anguish in her voice.

"Baby, you took him down to nothingness. He may still be alive but only in the barest sense of the word. He is existing between worlds," Alex said, brushing away a tear with his thumb.

"But he'll come back."

"Yes, he will. But not for some time, he won't have the strength. In any case, we'll be ready for him and we'll make sure he's completely destroyed," Alex said, his hand at her neck, touching her to soothe her.

* * * * *

As evening fell, Lee's father and the others came over with dinner and Aidan came downstairs, pulling her to him tightly and raining small kisses over her face. She sat between him and Alex and they all ate as they worked through the events of the night before.

Tante Elise had been home alone watching television when she'd noticed someone outside in the alley—a trash can was set on fire. She rushed outside to put it out and they hit her, knocking her out and taking her to the warehouse. Lee's father and brothers had learned that much from one of Angra's henchmen as he lay dying. Angra's plan had been to use her as a lure to get Lee, but she'd come early.

It appeared that a few of Angra's disciples had gotten away but from the sweep they did, but it looked like they'd cleared out of the city entirely. The local voodoo Priestess Vivianne had come by the shop earlier to declare she felt the city was clean and to thank the Charvez women for honoring the Compact.

Unfortunately, Lee knew that their struggle wasn't over. As long as Angra was out there somewhere, it would never be over. Breathing easy wasn't a luxury she was ready to afford herself just yet.

Chapter Eleven

Two weeks later, Lee stared out of the window of the limo and watched the lights in Times Square as she and Alex and Aidan drove to their hotel. Aidan had insisted that they leave New Orleans for a while for a vacation, to have some much-needed recuperation time. Additionally, his parents, grandmother and his sister and brothers had traveled to New York to meet Lee.

Alex had given notice at his job in Chicago and would be starting at Lee's uncle's financial services corporation at the end of the month. His family had taken the news less than enthusiastically. They had been browbeating him to stay in town for the sake of the family, to get married and have children. They refused to see that he was married in his heart when he shared a wife with another man, and Lee really couldn't blame them for it. It was hard enough for her to fathom.

"I love the Four Seasons, it's gorgeous and fit for a queen, and that means you," Alex said, leaning over to kiss the tip of her nose.

"It's all very overwhelming. What a huge city," she murmured, continuing to look out the window. They drove past Central Park and toward the hotel.

"We need to travel a lot more. Of course we'll go to Ireland this winter but perhaps a side trip to France afterwards, in the new year. I want to spoil you," Aidan said, kissing her hand where the ring that the three of them had designed sat, a large diamond bordered by gleaming sapphires.

"You already do spoil me, both of you. I ought to be ashamed." She laughed, not feeling the slightest bit ashamed or guilty.

"Traveling is romantic, sexy, fun. I can't believe you've never been to New York. We have so much to see and do in the next few days," Alex said.

The limo pulled into the drive of the Four Seasons and they all got out and went up to the palatial suite that Aidan had arranged for. Lee smiled, eyes alight like a kid on Christmas, as she saw the champagne on ice and the appetizer tray that were sitting on the low table in the living room.

Alex handed her a glass of champagne, frosty to the touch, and after she took a sip he slipped a chocolate-covered strawberry past her lips. Aidan knelt before her and slowly ran his hands up her thighs, murmuring in appreciation when he felt the thigh-high stockings she'd put on before leaving home. Alex unbuttoned her skirt and it fell to her feet and she stepped out of it.

Aidan's phone rang and he sighed, looking at the screen. "It's my brother, I have to take it. I'll be back," he said getting up and going into the other room to take the call.

"On your hands and knees," Alex said in a low commanding voice.

That voice never failed to make her wet and slightly dizzy. He gave a wicked chuckle, slowly unzipping his pants and letting his cock free of them. He leaned down, caught a trickle of cream that was rolling down her thigh and sucked it into his mouth.

"I haven't fucked your pretty little ass in over a week, I need to remedy that," he said, leaning down and licking the base of her spine. He reached out and untied her panties, slowly drawing them off, taking care to let the fabric brush over her engorged pussy as he did. She arched back with a moan and he teased her, rubbing the head of his cock over the swollen folds of her pussy, moving her moisture all over her sensitive skin.

"Please," she gasped out.

"Tell me what you want, baby," he said, slipping his hand under her shirt and rolling her nipple between his fingers. The other hand slid back, gathering moisture from her weeping slit, and wet fingers pressed into her anus.

"Please fuck me," she gasped out.

"Here?" He dipped the head of his cock into her slightly. "Or here?" He moved up and slowly pushed his cock into her tight rear passage that he'd moistened with her own juices.

She whimpered and arched back, taking more of him inside of her. "Right there," she groaned.

"You're so fucking hot, so smooth and tight," he ground out as he slid the rest of the way inside of her. He moved a hand to her pussy, slowly tracing her lips, over her clit and into her gate, matching the rhythm of his movements into her ass. "I love this, I love the way you feel around me."

Lee did too. At first it had been slightly uncomfortable for her. The idea of anal sex was not something she'd thought of as normal. But Alex loved it so much, he took his time as he stroked his hands over her body, covering her with his own, dominating her with his size. She'd begun to be turned on by the very idea of it, the sheer naughtiness of it and she loved how much pleasure it gave Alex, especially when she had both of them inside of her at once. She knew how much each man loved the feel of the heads of their cocks stroking over the other as they thrust within her. She knew that their curiosity about the other was slowly building and she couldn't wait to see it when it finally happened.

Aidan came back into the room and she watched him pull his pants and boxers off then stalk toward them, his cock so hard it was flush against the flesh of his stomach. He knelt before her and made to move under her, to enter her and she stopped him by taking him into her mouth instead, her hands on his thighs for balance.

"Yes," he hissed and caressed her neck and face, finally clutching her hair in his fists as he rode her mouth.

Alex slapped the bare skin of her ass and she gave a squeal of surprise, but the warm tingling it left behind was less than painful. He ran his fingers over the spot he'd slapped lovingly. "So pretty," he said with a grunt. "You like that, don't you?"

She hummed around a mouthful of Aidan's cock, her eyes sliding closed. Alex slapped her on the other side and the fingers he had in her pussy quickened their pace, strumming over her clit.

Aidan leaned down and grabbed Lee's wrist, the bloodlust long since having taken over, and struck, watching her fingers open and close helplessly as her orgasm hit, causing her to scream around him and arch into Alex's strokes.

Alex gave a grunt and slammed into her once, twice and a third time and stilled as his cock shot his cum into her with a long groan from deep within his throat.

Aidan opened his link between the other two and their pleasure slammed into him. That, combined with the velvet intoxication of Lee's blood, caused him to come deep into Lee's throat.

The three of them collapsed onto the lush carpeting of the floor, panting and boneless.

* * * * *

The next days were a blur. Aidan's parents were gracious and it was clear they adored Aidan and in turn, Lee. They'd taken her, and the unconventional situation, into their lives with open arms. His sister and her mate were warm and welcoming as were his brothers.

Lee had been the most nervous about meeting Aidan's grandmother. It was clear by how he spoke of her and the number of times a week they spoke on the phone that they were close and she wanted very desperately for the older woman to like her, in no small part because of how much stock Aidan put in his grandmother's opinion.

When they'd walked into the suite where his grandmother was staying a tall, lithe woman with silvery hair down to her waist approached her, her head tilted to the side as she took Lee in from head to toe.

A smile came over her face and her gold-flecked hazel eyes danced. "You must be Lee." She took Lee's hands in her own. "I am so glad to meet you. You have made Aidan so happy. So lovely too! Powerful." She kissed Lee's cheeks and stood back. "Welcome to our family."

In relief, Lee let out the breath she'd been holding. "Thank you so much! I've been so anxious to meet you, Aidan and Alex both can't say enough wonderful things about you. They didn't say that you were absolutely gorgeous though." And she was. She certainly didn't look like any grandmother Lee had ever seen in her faded jeans and tee shirt.

His grandmother laughed and grabbed Aidan in a hug. "She's going to fit into our family just fine."

* * * * *

They had dinners at swanky restaurants. Alex and Lee went shopping and sightseeing during the days and they learned some new things about their bond from Aidan's father.

Apparently, because Lee was such a powerful witch, the conversion was happening, but at a very slow rate. It would be at least a hundred years before she would need to take blood occasionally to live and probably one hundred and fifty until the sunlight began to bother her in any great measure. She would gain a long lifespan and the strength and speed of vampires but not the ability to shapeshift, or at least the other witches hadn't ever been able to. Aidan's father felt that the rate of her conversion was directly connected to her power level, the more powerful the witch, the slower the conversion would be.

Alex would not be affected like Lee was, though. Only full conversion would enable him to have the gifts that Lee was receiving, although because he was bonded to Aidan as well and they exchanged blood occasionally, his lifespan would be lengthened. Aidan and Lee knew that they'd have to discuss that issue more in depth later on.

Chapter Twelve

The trip was relaxing and when they got back to New Orleans at the end of the week, Lee laden down with packages, she was glad that they'd gone. Not only because she'd enjoyed Aidan's family so much but because she'd needed the time away to let herself heal a bit.

Lee had gone back to work at the shop and was continuing her lessons with her mother now that *tante* Elise was gone.

One night, a few weeks after they'd returned from New York, Alex and Aidan were discussing how to best protect Lee. She'd come home and stood in the hallway, listening as Aidan and Alex spoke.

"We are going to have to find him, you know. He won't just leave Lee alone. He'll come back as soon as he can build up the strength, bent on revenge," Alex said to Aidan as they had a glass of wine together.

"I know, I just wanted her to have a few months without worry. Where we could settle into a routine. She deserves some normalcy." Aidan sighed heavily. The entire issue had been weighing on his mind.

"We could leave, move to another city. We could go back to Chicago, my family could help protect her."

Aidan laughed. "You really think Lee would live on the Carter compound with guard dogs and wizard bodyguards? You think she'd leave New Orleans and her family?"

Lee gave a mental snort at that idea.

"No. We could team up and push her into it."

Ha! Lee thought.

"Alex, you're seriously delusional if you think that she'd allow us to push her into any decision. Well, any decision that doesn't involve sex anyway. But you do need to deal with your family, you can't let this go on." Lee smirked from her position in the hall.

Alex exhaled agitatedly. "How do you suggest I do that? Should I give in and marry Beth Pickney of the Chicago Pickneys? Have two children with her and live a mile from my parents? Go to the country club every Sunday for brunch? You think Lee would go for that?" he said, laughing.

"No. I think you should marry Lee. I am already married to her under the law and custom of my people. You can give her the human marriage ceremony, bind yourselves in that way. It will give her another layer of protection and also legitimize your relationship with her in the eyes of your family."

"You'd give that up for me? You already asked her, she already said yes."

"I won't be giving anything up. We *are* married. Anyway, I skirt the basic legalities of existence. If she's legitimately your wife under human law, she's protected should anything happen to either of us. If I die, the laws of my people will protect her rights, she'd inherit all of my property and my family would shelter her. If you did, the same goes, but only if you were legally married."

Lee realized just how much she didn't deserve Aidan for the thousandth time.

Alex leaned over and hugged Aidan. "Thank you. Thank you for being the best friend I've ever had, for being my brother and thank you for bringing Lee into my life. It's an honor to share her with you."

Lee waited a few minutes and noisily came in the door and waved to the two men sitting in the living room. "Don't you two look like you're up to no good?" she said teasingly. It had taken a while but the smile was back in her voice and she had let go of the grief and guilt over Elise's death.

"Come and sit here with us," Aidan said silkily and she raised a brow but plopped down on the couch between them. He brought her hand to his mouth and ran his tongue between her knuckles, causing her eyelids to drop to half-mast. "You know that you and I are married in the eyes and the law of my culture, yes?" Lee nodded and kissed his chin.

"Busted. I admit it. I was listening in the hall," she admitted with a smile.

Alex turned her head to face him. "Such a naughty girl."

"Mmm, very. Will you punish me later?" she asked, thrilled to watch his pupils darken and widen as he smirked.

"Definitely," he growled and she smirked.

She looked at Aidan. "And this is okay with you?"

He laughed and kissed her deeply until she was boneless and very horny. "Yes, I'm perfectly all right with it. Alex and I have worked this out between us thoroughly. I am totally secure in our bond, in our marriage. I didn't even need the human ceremony but wanted to do it for you."

"Okay. Well, my family has been amazingly progressive with this whole threesome deal so let's do it. I'd like to keep it small though. Alex, would you like to invite your parents? I know things have been hard between you and them lately, but this could perhaps convince them that you are in this for the long haul."

"Yes, very much. In fact, if it's all right with you, I'd like to have the ceremony in Chicago. I know it's a lot to ask but my mother is frail and I don't think she'd handle the trip down here very well. Your family is welcome to stay at my family's estate. We can fly all of them up, that's not a problem."

She felt a small pang of regret for not being able to have the wedding in New Orleans but it really wasn't so much for Alex to ask. "All right. You have given up a lot to be here, this isn't such a big sacrifice for me."

"I've gotten far more than I've given up," he said. "We can do a reception here when we get back, you know, a big party with family and friends."

"That sounds good. Let's do it then."

They decided that they'd do it in three weeks time. Alex's mother wasn't thrilled at the short timeline but they wanted to keep things small and intimate and Alex knew if he gave his mother more time she'd turn it into a society page event with five hundred people.

Chapter Thirteen

Aidan and Lee took his lavish private jet to Chicago three weeks later. He sat curled around her, stroking a languid hand over her spine.

She stretched, catlike, and turned to face him. "So you seem pretty used to this whole life of luxury thing. Private jet, champagne on ice, limo taking us to the airport…"

He gave her a wicked smile. "It is nice though, isn't it? Let me tell you, things weren't so nice in the eighteenth and nineteenth centuries. It took days by coach or horse, traveling at night, to get anywhere. No cell phones, no indoor plumbing, no double head showers. No women like you."

"Well, you do spoil me so and I love it. My family didn't have to come out first-class, you know. My father had a conniption when I gave them all the tickets yesterday."

He laughed. "It really isn't an issue. They are your family, Alex and I want them to be treated well." He shrugged as if it were an everyday occurrence to fly out fifteen people first-class.

"Well, I'm ever so grateful," she said suggestively, her hand sliding up his thigh.

"Is that right?" he responded, his voice thickening, eyes bleeding to amber.

She got to her knees and he opened up his thighs to admit her. Slowly, she slid his zipper down until his cock sprang free and she rubbed her cheek along it. He made a sort of purr at the back of his throat, hands slowly stroking over her face and hair. She pulled his pants off and settled back in between his legs.

She took him into her mouth inch by inch, savoring the taste of him, the salt and musk of him sang out to her as he filled her senses.

"Mmmm, yes, that's so good," he said softly. She hummed in appreciation and his head fell back against the couch.

She kissed down his length and flicked her tongue over his balls, gently taking each one into her mouth and reveling in the way his thighs trembled as she did it. She slid her hand up her thigh and under the already soaking panties she was wearing and wet herself with her honey. Using her lube, she slowly tickled his bottom until he spread his legs wider and scooted toward her, giving her access to him. She gave him a heated look and he watched as she slowly worked a finger inside of him. Impossibly, he hardened more and gave a deep groan of pleasure when she found his prostate and began to stroke over it in time with the movements of her mouth over his cock.

He began to pump his hips upward to meet her, his head slowly moving from side to side as his climax approached. The hands in her hair were tight now as he slipped into the Irish brogue that he used when upset or passionate. He was murmuring encouragement and making wordless grunts, whimpers and groans. Suddenly, the muscles of his anus clamped down on her fingers and he thrust up hard, shooting his cum deep into her throat for what felt like minutes.

She kissed and licked him until he had gone soft then pulled off gently with a parting kiss on his belly button.

"Jaysus, Lee," he said breathlessly.

She chuckled and straightened first his and then her clothing and sat back beside him, drinking her champagne and stroking his hair.

"What did I do before I met you?" he asked softly.

"You had donors," she said dryly.

He sat up and pulled her onto his lap, facing him. He slipped the buttons on her blouse open and gazed at her breasts, unbound, the way he liked them. Idly, he stroked his thumbs across them. "There is no comparison, my jealous dove. I certainly never experienced half of what you and I just shared with anyone before I found you. Sure, I love sex, but sex with a mate is monumental. Sex with you makes the sex I had in the centuries before you came along seem horrible by comparison. I can certainly say I've never had a finger up my bum before, that was…surprising. But quite nice. I'm guessing it was an inspiration from Alex."

She nodded and tried to laugh but ended up on a moan as he scraped over a nipple with his incisors. "I'm glad you liked it," she managed to get out as she panted. "I know you're curious about Alex," she added.

"Curious, yes."

"Would it be the first time?"

"That I was curious?"

She shot him a glare and he laughed. "No, I've been with a man before a time or two. Not really my cup of tea. On the other hand, this bond between us makes things different."

She shivered, imagining them stroking each other, already knowing how sexy it was as they kissed or touched her, fingers and mouths brushing against the other's when they were all together.

"Please don't let me hold you back," she said with a grin and he laughed again.

"We'll see," was all he'd say.

The pilot announced over the intercom that they'd be touching down in twenty minutes. "I'd better get moving then, hmmm?" Aidan murmured as his fingers found their way into her panties and slipped into her moist pussy. He slipped two inside of her and she rode him while he licked and bit her nipples, finally feeding from her while he flicked his middle finger up and across her clit over and over.

She arched her breasts into his face as she rode his hand, holding onto his shoulders for balance. When he closed the wound with a sweep of his tongue he pulled her to his lips to kiss her passionately. She could taste her blood, rich and metallic on his tongue and it mixed with his taste, salty and spicy. They both groaned as the fasten seatbelt sign came on and they had to separate as the flight attendant would be coming back through any minute.

She almost came again as he licked his fingers and drank the last of his champagne before handing the glass to the steward. He was so sexy. He was smooth and lean and sensual and he took his time with everything he did. It had been nice to have the last several days alone with him again and she decided that every year she'd take separate vacations with each of her mates to get that alone time.

* * * * *

Alex met them at the airport with a car to pick them up and take them back to his condo on Lake Shore Drive. She was pretty much in awe when she walked in the door. The walls were covered with expensive art, the views were incredible and the furnishings and appliances were all very top of the line. "Yeesh, you gave this up to live in a Greek Revival in New Orleans?" she asked as she sat down on a couch.

"I gave up a life of loneliness to have a life filled with love and fellowship. This place is nice but I never really *lived* here. Now I live with my two best friends." He shrugged. "I love our house. Although I am having my electronics shipped down. I'll keep a small apartment here in town for visits but there's no use keeping this giant place and leaving all of the stuff here."

"God forbid you should only have three thirty-two inch televisions instead of this six-foot-high monster," she muttered with amusement as she went to wash up. She was tired. The last several days had been very long and very full of activity. She'd finished a painting that she'd done on commission, helped at the shop and had been dealing with Alex's mother and sisters over the phone with wedding plans.

She'd just finished drying her face and was undoing her hair when she heard him come into the room.

"I missed you," Alex said gruffly as he came into the bathroom and stood behind her. She shivered with anticipation and moisture pooled in her pussy as she heard his zipper come down and the buckle on his belt jingle. Without preamble, her skirt was pushed up and her panties shoved down and his cock slammed into her.

She arched her back, gasping at the feel of his thick cock, so different from Aidan's longer shaft, filling her up, hitting nerves that hadn't been fired since the morning he'd gone a week before.

"That's right, baby, so hot and wet. Like a fist." He grunted, his pace picking up, no other sound but the slap of wet flesh against wet flesh. He pulled her blouse off, a few buttons flying off and hitting the floor. "I love to watch your tits bounce while I fuck you," he said into her ear. "Touch them," he ordered.

She leaned her head back onto his shoulder and watched the incredibly erotic picture in the mirror as his hand worked her pussy and her hands worked her nipples. "Oh god. I'm coming," she wailed and her body clamped down on him, causing a surprised grunt to come from him.

"Yes! Milk my cock," he muttered as he slammed into her so hard that the bottles on the shelves were clinking together. He threw his head back and gave a hoarse shout and she felt his cock pulse as he came.

He pulled out slowly and kissed her spine. "Sorry about the blouse," he said, giving her an unrepentant smile in the mirror.

She snorted. "This is the sixth one you've ruined."

"I told you, buy yourself as many as you need, on me. Anyway, I felt your pussy gush that sweet cream when I did it, so don't pretend it doesn't work for you," he said with a laugh.

* * * * *

The next day they headed out to Alex's familial home. Lee was slightly envious of Aidan, who got to stay back at the condo and sleep while she had to go and face Alex's parents.

Lee's family had arrived that morning and they were all to have brunch together at the Carters' home. She was nervous, she hoped that they were being treated well, although she knew they'd stand up for themselves if they had to, but she also wanted his parents to accept her, despite the less than typical circumstances that they were operating under.

When they pulled up to the high iron gates that swung open and drove up the long scenic drive that ended with a house—well, if you could call what was most likely at least twelve thousand square feet of perfectly decorated, three-storied mansion with Italian marble floors and exquisitely manicured grounds a house—she turned to him with a raised eyebrow.

"My god! You grew up here? It's a palace."

Alex shrugged. "It never occurred to me that everyone didn't live this way until I went off to college."

"It's beautiful. It must have been like a fairy tale growing up here."

He pulled her into his side, his arm around her shoulders. "Fairy tale might be a stretch. You know, my parents aren't the most demonstrative emotionally. I think I've heard 'I love you' more from you than I did my entire life until we met. But in their own way they love me and my brothers and sisters."

"I can't imagine what they'll think of my family," she said, knowing that her family couldn't go more than five minutes without a kiss or a hug or an "I love you".

"I think your family is wonderful. How could anyone else not think the same?" he said reassuringly. Privately, he hoped his own family would learn a few things from the Charvezes.

They walked to the front doors and she felt the spells protecting the house. A man in uniform came, pulled the wards away and led them inside.

"Mr. Alex, it is good to have you home again," the man said with quiet dignity.

"Thank you, Peterson. This is Amelia Charvez, my fiancée. Lee, this is Peterson. He's been working here since I was a child."

The man gave her a bow and a smile. "It is a pleasure to meet you, Miss. Your family arrived only a short while ago, they are all in the morning room with the Carters having some brunch. I'll see you through."

The house was as impressive inside as out but it lacked the warmth of their house, or that of the house she'd grown up in. The marble was cool and regal, the art and arranged flowers more for perfection than an expression of the tastes of the people that owned the house.

Alex and Lee entered the room and her mother and sister looked up, smiled, and got to their feet to greet them. Lee gave them a hug and kiss. "I see you got here all right."

"Oh yes, the flight was perfect. Thank you for the cars that picked us up at the airport, by the way," her mother said with a smile at Alex, but Lee could see the stress lines around her mouth and put her guard up.

"Lee, honey?" Alex said, getting her attention.

"Oh, I'm sorry," she said, turning to him and giving him her complete attention so that she could meet his parents.

He kissed her temple to reassure her. "Amelia Charvez, this is my father Giles Carter and my mother, Cheryl. Mom, Dad, this is Lee." Alex indicated a tall, regal man with salt-and-pepper hair and then the woman in the expensive suit standing next to him.

The man shook her hand and gave her an assessing glance. Lee felt him examining her, testing her power, but she shut him out quickly and effortlessly. Wizards might do such things to people but witches didn't unless they were faced with a threat. He winced and took a step back, his eyes wide for a moment.

Alex's mother was tall and birdlike. Indeed, she looked every inch the fragile woman that Alex had described. She gave Lee an assessing glance of her own but this was more of a check to see if she'd be worthy of trotting out as their new daughter-in-law. Lee shook her hand gingerly, afraid she'd crush the other woman's bones.

The rest of the afternoon was an experience. It wasn't as if they were mean or rude to her, Alex's father seemed to have learned his lesson after the magical slap she'd given him for attempting to probe her, but they weren't very friendly. The men that were there had a coolly dismissive attitude toward witches and Lee and the other Charvez women gritted their teeth through it all. The women were aloof. Alex's older sister was the exception. She was especially nice and actually warm as they discussed the wedding schedule for the next day. Lee's mother did her best to put Alex's at ease but Lee heaved a sigh of relief when it was all over and they could leave to go and get ready for the rehearsal dinner.

* * * * *

"I'm sorry, I could feel how uncomfortable you were," Alex said as they got back to the condo where Aidan had just awoken.

"I wasn't exactly uncomfortable. It's just that we are very different. I'm sure they are just as eager as I am to find a way to bridge the gap," Lee said, kissing him gently. She could feel how embarrassed he was and she didn't want to add to his guilt over his parents' behavior.

She showered, not objecting at all when Aidan slipped into the giant glass-enclosed stall to grab a quick sip. She put on the deep blue cocktail dress she and Em had picked up the week before and the ridiculously spiky shoes that went with it.

Both men gave her an appreciative look when she came into the living room where they were waiting for her.

Dinner was in an impressively posh restaurant and Lee was reminded again what a different world she came from compared to Aidan and Alex, who took this sort of place for granted.

They drank champagne and ate wonderful food. Lee met more members of Alex's family—the rest of his brothers, minus the one who'd gone to his grandfather's faction, his aunts and uncles and several old school friends as well. They all eyed her with curiosity.

Lee realized through the evening that Alex was the golden boy and that she was being seen by some as an interloper. Chicago society and wizarding community alike considered him to be quite the catch. Judging by the looks she was getting and the conversations she'd overheard, the non-magical people wondered why a gorgeous and successful guy like him would be marrying a short red-haired girl from New Orleans and the magical folk were assessing her power level. She'd been working hard with her mother to shield herself from others, knowing that if people could look at her and see just how powerful she truly was there would be trouble everywhere she went.

After midnight she looked up and noticed that Alex and Aidan, along with the majority of the male guests, had gone. They were both nearby, she could feel them through the link, and she sent out a quick questioning burst.

"Where is your father?" Lee's mother asked.

"They're in the lounge, smoking cigars and drinking cognac." Lee rolled her eyes.

Her mother laughed and touched her arm. Alex's mother was on the other side of the room speaking with two other equally frail and birdlike women. The Charvez women decided to escape and go out on the verandah for some fresh air.

Once out there though, dread began to sneak up Lee's spine. "Something's here, *maman*," she said quietly.

"I know." Her mother moved so that she and Lee were able to link hands and share power. She sent out a mental call to Alex and Aidan and felt them moving toward her.

"Hello. You must be my sister-in-law to be."

Lee looked at the tall, raven-haired man who was leaning in the doorway, ankles crossed. He was spilling power everywhere. A peacock display, she thought with annoyance.

"You must be Alex's brother, Peter. I don't believe you were invited," Lee said curtly. She looked him over curiously, so this was the brother who'd left and taken Alex into the dark path.

She could feel him trying to probe her defenses and she let her shields down partially, let her power shine, and his eyes widened and he stepped back.

"What is it with wizards anyway? It's rude to go barging in where you aren't invited," Lee said, referring to his mental invasion and his party-crashing at the same time.

"Well, aren't you just full of surprises? Such a little thing to possess so much power. He said you were strong."

Lee sighed, sounding bored. "It's not the size but what you do with what you've got. Men can never seem to get that through their heads. Now, why don't you be on your way before Alex gets out here and we can pretend this meeting never even happened."

"Aren't you the bossy one?" Peter said, white teeth gleaming with his smile.

Before Lee could answer she felt Alex and Aidan approach and turned toward the doors. "Peter, what are you doing here?" Alex said on a near growl as he came out onto the verandah. He looked at Lee long enough to be assured that she wasn't harmed in any way and put his arm around her shoulders.

"I just came to deliver our congratulations. Grandfather and our uncle were disappointed not to get an invitation to your wedding. I was just getting acquainted with your bride-to-be." He clucked his tongue at his brother. "Tsk tsk, brother dear, why didn't you tell us she was more than an ordinary witch?"

Aidan stepped out then with one of Alex's younger brothers and moved to her other side, subtly putting Lee's mother behind him.

"Peter, you need to be leaving now," Alex said to his oldest brother, his power crackling through the air. "You made your choice over twenty years ago. If Mom or Dad see you here it'll just cause more upset."

Lee could feel Peter's power building up. Focusing, she sent out her own power and latched onto his, draining it away from him and pulling it back into herself. All three Carter men looked at her, shocked.

"What?" she asked with an innocent flutter of her eyelashes.

Alex wanted to laugh but he held back.

Peter narrowed his eyes with menace. "This isn't over, Alex. You had real power and position with us. It's lowering to see that you walked away from that to come back to these petty magicians with their puny power. But this wife of yours, now she's a real asset to our family. Alex, think of your children, think of the wizards she'll breed for us if you come home where you belong."

Lee snorted. "I'm not a brood mare. What's more, I certainly don't have any plans to have my power corrupted so take your little dark magic tricks and hit the road."

Aidan chuckled, the sound like warm honey in the evening air. "She's not yours, dark mage. Even if she wasn't powerful enough to grind you into dust with a thought, she's bound to me and to Alex."

"This isn't over, vampire," Peter sneered in disgust but backed away. "You know we won't just let you and this witch slip away, Alex. Grandfather wants you to come back home where you belong. Bring this woman and your power and you'll have everything you've ever dreamed of," he said and turned, stalking away.

"Welcome to the family," Alex's younger brother said, taking her hand and kissing it gallantly. "I mean that, I am honored to have you as a sister-in-law."

Lee laughed inwardly at the ridiculousness of the fact that it was a magical pissing contest that had finally won the respect of part of Alex's family. She smiled at him and they all relaxed as they heard Peter's car speed out of the parking lot.

Chapter Fourteen

Peter stormed into the house, pushing past his uncle and up the stairs into his grandfather's study.

"I take it that you weren't able to convince Alex to come back to the fold," George Carter said, fingers steepled before him.

"He's as stubborn as ever. The woman though, she's everything Damian said and more. She's very powerful and it didn't take any visible effort on her part to summon her power or control it. She threw off my probes pretty easily. It appears that she's linked to Alex somehow, they share power."

"Is that so?" His grandfather got a gleam in his eye and leaned forward, very interested. "Think of the great-grandchildren she'd bear for me with Alex's power bound to hers. Wizards of immense power and witches, too. We'd build this family back to its former glory, what we were like before the weaklings took over."

"Damian wants her for himself," Peter said, throwing himself into a chair.

"I don't give a damn what he wants, he's just some weak magician who thinks he can demand things, we'll show him when it's time.

"I've got you and your cousin but that's it. The rest of us are all old men. We need more males to carry on our line or this family will finally move to the path of light and *we'll* be the minority. I can't have that. No, you need to get that wife of yours pregnant and soon and we need to bring Alex and his bride over to us."

"That vampire is involved. He says that she's bound to him and Alex. I wasn't able to probe enough to know if it's true."

"Really? Interesting, but nothing insurmountable. We'll kill him and take his power for our own when the time comes."

"And Damian?"

"Oh yes, we'll kill him too. He's got immense power to feed on. But not right yet. He's got information that we don't about the witch. Best to play along with him, let him think we'll let him have her once we get Alex back."

"I'll work with the others to grab Alex and the witch," Peter said, standing up.

"Yes, you do that. Good work, boy."

Peter inclined his head and left the room.

Chapter Fifteen

The wedding was at sunset and went off without a single problem. The dress fit perfectly, a deep blue sheath with hand beading at the gently curved neckline and up the side slit. It wasn't the traditional white but they were far from the traditional couple. Aidan stood tall as Alex's best man and both looked handsome in their perfectly tailored tuxedos. Em was her maid of honor and the cream-colored silk mid-thigh dress with the wrap front showed off her long, lean form.

The group was gorgeous and everyone had a great time. Alex did throw his mother a dirty look when a reporter and photographer from the society page showed up and took pictures but Lee just squeezed his hand and sent him patience.

Afterwards, the reception was flowing with the same good food and champagne that they'd been enjoying over the last two days. She danced with everyone and it appeared that Alex's father had softened up a bit toward her after all.

"I heard about your meeting with my eldest son last night," he said quietly as they danced.

"Yes, well…" she said and stopped, not quite knowing what to say, after all, the man had lost a son.

"Alex says you've got quite the power behind those shields."

"If you have a question, you should ask it," she said bluntly.

"You're angry that I tried to probe your power yesterday."

"Tried and failed, but yes. I don't know all there is to know about wizard culture but in my culture such behavior is considered rude and disrespectful."

He laughed then. "You have spine, I like that. You don't take any crap. You're strong and willing to stand up for him in the face of his brother and my father. Those are qualities I can respect. You're an exceptional woman, Lee, and I can see why my son is willing to share you with another.

"As for the probe, I should apologize but I'm not going to. It's rude in our culture too, but I couldn't just let you barge into my family without knowing your motivations. Alex is my son." He shrugged.

"Then why not ask me? I love Alex, he loves me. I respect him and his power, he respects mine. He's a grown man, Mr. Carter, and a very strong-willed one, it's not like I could have made him do anything he didn't want to do."

"Okay, so why has my son left us again to move to New Orleans? He's now hours away from his rightful place at my side as ruler of this family."

She nodded. "Isn't that the proper way of things? That children create their own lives with wives and husbands? Not that they turn their backs on their family but that they create a new branch? He hasn't *left* you, he moved to be with his wife. Surely you can see the difference."

"He can't rule from New Orleans."

"Of course he can, if that's what he chooses to do."

"And does he? Choose to rule?"

She put her palm on his chest. "Oh no, Mr. Carter, that's something you need to take up with Alex. I'm happy to let you ask about things that pertain to me and my motivations but Alex's are his own to share or not as he sees fit. If he hasn't shared that with you and you've already asked him, that is his choice. You know your son, no one can make him do anything."

"There were those who did, once."

"But I'd argue that that was Alex's choice, he made it of his free will. Oh sure, he was manipulated. His Grandfather worked the fact that Alex was full of ego and young and eager to prove himself. But Alex wasn't forced into the dark path against his wishes, just as he didn't come back to the path of light against his wishes. He's a very strong person, can you not see that?"

"I see that I've lost one son to my father and brother. Alex is the next oldest, the next in line for all intents and purposes, and I won't have him turn his back on us for a cheap thrill."

"So now I'm a cheap thrill?" She laughed, incredulous. "Neither Aidan nor I will ever make Alex do anything he doesn't want to do. His being with me is his choice, one that he made freely."

"And now he's left Chicago to move down there. The son that came back to me has now left again."

"Not you, I want you to see that very important fact." She paused and cocked her head at him. "Tell me something, Mr. Carter, when Alex lived in Chicago, how many times a week did you see him?"

"I can't see what that has to do with anything."

She smiled and patted his arm. "Then you aren't looking very hard. I'm not trying to steal Alex away from his roots. He came back to you because he sees your path as the right one, doesn't that tell you something? I appreciate what you are and who you are. When we have children, if they are male, they will be raised with an understanding and appreciation of their background as wizards and will be trained as such. Alex will be keeping an apartment here and we plan to visit often. Perhaps this bit of distance can be a good thing, maybe you and he can work on being closer in emotional ways instead of just geographical. It's not like you don't have the money to fly down any time you wish and you've been told that you are welcome in our home and if that doesn't suit, there are a number of fine hotels in New Orleans."

Alex's father looked at her, taking her measure, and nodded shortly. "Well, you've won my other children over, too. I suppose I'll just be the next in a long line of conquests." He smiled, and she finally saw a real resemblance between father and son. The smile soon dimmed though. "I should tell you that I am concerned that my father has taken an interest in you and Alex, watch your back."

"Thank you, I'm watching it as well as Alex's and Aidan's."

"It appears I've underestimated witches for far too long. Welcome to the family, Lee," he said and kissed her cheek.

Alex had been watching the interlude with interest. He could feel what Lee was feeling so he knew his father had insulted her, annoyed her and made her angry but she'd refused to back down but had also remained diplomatic instead of losing her temper, all because she loved him.

Aidan had watched as well, holding Alex back a few times when he wanted to go and interfere. "She's handling herself just fine, Alex, let her do this. Your father needs to hear a few things," he murmured and Alex held back.

After the evening wore down they headed back to the condo after saying their goodbyes to everyone. Lee's family would be returning to New Orleans on Aidan's jet the next morning and Lee and the guys would be heading back the following day. They would all take a honeymoon in the fall in Italy but Alex had to be back at work by Tuesday.

Back at the condo, Aidan reached out to unlock the doors when a feeling of intense dread hit Lee. "Something is wrong," she said and started to throw out a spell of protection—but it was too late.

Chapter Sixteen

She awoke slowly, feeling like she was wrapped in cotton. She realized she'd been drugged. Lying in a narrow bed, she realized that she wasn't tied down but that the room was locked and stripped pretty bare and lacked windows. She shivered as it occurred to her that the room was as good as a cell.

She opened her link to Alex and Aidan. Aidan was very far away. It was daylight and he'd managed to get inside the condo where he was safe. He'd told Alex's family and her own about the kidnapping and they were out looking for them. The women were using spells, as were the wizards, and the non-magical relatives were scouring George Carter's various holdings trying to find traces of them there.

Reaching out, Lee could feel Alex nearby but not conscious yet. Other than that, he was healthy and she breathed a sigh of relief.

Find out what you can, darlin,' we're looking but we need the help, Aidan sent out. She could feel his worry and his anger that anyone dared harm her. Thanking the goddess for her gifts, she slipped her physical form and sent her consciousness out to take a look around. The problem was that she didn't know Chicago very well so she couldn't tell Aidan much. She walked in the minds of the men who were sitting outside of the room where she was being held and saw — confirming their suspicions — that they worked for Alex's grandfather and sent that knowledge back to Aidan. They hadn't been told a whole lot so she couldn't garner much more information.

She found Alex and walked into his mind, bringing him to consciousness. He was unharmed but would continue feigning unconsciousness until they could get a better idea of what they were facing.

She heard noises in the hall and stayed in a corner of Alex's mind as three men entered his room.

"You're sure he's not hurt?" a silver-haired man asked.

My grandfather. Peter is with him and my, my, my, so is Angra, Alex sent silently along the link. A shiver of dread and fury worked down Lee's spine.

"We used more on him than the woman, he's much larger, but the doctors assure me he will come out of it within the next ten minutes or so. The woman might already be awake," Alex's brother assured his grandfather.

"Let me have her, you promised her to me!" Angra demanded and Lee felt Alex's fury rise.

"You'll get what's coming to you, all in good time. We need her for the time being though, Damian, so don't think about messing this up," Peter growled at him.

Lee found it interesting that Alex's grandfather and brother treated the dark mage so casually. A mental smile formed as she realized that they had no idea of just who exactly Angra was, or that he was more powerful than they were. Tucking that away for the time, hoping she could use it to their advantage, Lee turned her attention back to what was happening in Alex's room.

"Let's go and check on her, we can use her to gain Alex's compliance," his brother said.

Lee loosed herself from Alex and slipped back into her body. She laid a subtle spell of protection from compulsion over both herself and Alex and sat up, noticing she still had on her dress from the reception. Oh she was pissed when she saw that it was ruined, that dress cost her two hundred bucks! Ignoring Alex's amused snort in her head, she checked that Aidan was still along the link and he was, she felt his extreme agitation and upset at his inability to be out helping.

The door opened and the men came in, a bit surprised that she was awake and waiting. She thanked the goddess that wizards were so arrogant that they knew little of what a witch dreamer was capable of, because as long as they underestimated her she had the upper hand.

"You're awake," George Carter said with a smarmy smile. He turned to the guard outside. "Bring my granddaughter some breakfast." The man scurried off.

"Don't bother, I don't plan to be here long. You must be Alex's *grandpere*. I wish I could say it was nice to meet you but you did drug and kidnap me and that tends to make me less than sociable. I take it you have Alex and Aidan, too?"

"Alex is here and is well. Your vampire managed to elude us but that doesn't matter, he's not important."

She smirked. "You want to tell me why you decided to go all commando and kidnap us?"

She felt him try to push past her shields but she kept them tight against him. She felt his frustration. "You're strong. No matter, I'm stronger," he said arrogantly.

She sighed in annoyance and her eyes narrowed when Angra came into the room. *Hold back the anger, it will contaminate your magic*, she heard *tante* Elise's admonition in her brain, recalling a lesson from childhood. With some difficulty she tamped it down, managing to think constructively.

Alex's grandfather sat down on the edge of the bed and Peter leaned on the doorjamb while Angra paced. "My dear, I'm afraid you have let the biases of my son and the rest of those do-gooders taint your perception of me. I'm not a bad man, I love my grandson and as you're his wife, my fondness extends to you as well. I just want him, and you, of course, here with me and mine where you belong. Surely you can understand that."

"I understand that Alex has his own mind. He made his choice of his own free will when he came to you and then later when he left you fifteen years ago. Where he comes and goes is up to him."

"Surely you can influence him. After all, my strong grandson is actually sharing you with another man, or rather, a vampire. I can't understand why but there it is."

"I love Alex, I wouldn't ever use my magic to influence him. Why don't you ask him why instead of me?"

He'd tried to bend her with compulsion but she understood and felt comforted by the fact that her magic was stronger than that of anyone in the room. She cast the compulsion off, let it flow over her like water flowing over a rock.

"Damian said you were strong."

She smirked at his ignorance and shot Angra a look, sharing that moment with him. Letting him think she was on his side.

A man brought her breakfast on a tray into the room and placed it on a table. She could smell the drugs laced into it and sneered. "Take it away. You know, you could really use some etiquette lessons on how to be a proper host. I want to see Alex and know he's okay."

"The food isn't drugged."

"Bullshit. I can smell it. We witches can smell such things, you know, it's a handy talent. The hashbrowns are laced with a narcotic to induce sleep, the coffee and juice as well."

"Sir, your grandson is awake and demanding to see you," a guard said as he entered the room.

Alex's grandfather stood up. "Bring her along, I want Alex to know she's unharmed. He can be quite strong when he's angry."

Two huge men grabbed her upper arms and carried her down the hall in his wake. The door to Alex's room was unlocked and she shook off the guards and went to him, letting him embrace her tightly. He kissed her forehead and frowned darkly at the bruises beginning to form on her upper arms.

"You have harmed my wife, Grandfather," he said, the room crackling with his power.

"Hold on, love, don't let him win," she said quietly.

"I apologize, Alex, I didn't realize the guards were holding her that tightly. It won't happen again. As I was trying to explain to your lovely wife, our last intention is to hurt either one of you. We just want you to come back home where you belong."

Alex urged her, through the link, to keep on trying to find out where they were. She sat quietly in Alex's arms and slipped her body, gliding quietly into his brother's subconscious to see if she could get answers.

She sent the pictures she took from his mind through the link so that Aidan and Alex could see them. She also saw that they'd been the ones to restore Angra to his power and that they planned to kill him when they had used him all they could. She wanted to laugh out loud at their foolish arrogance but started working on a way to use it instead.

She slipped into Angra and felt his emotions roiling around. There was a hint of something she couldn't quite grasp or see. Someone else?

Alex's grandfather was still attempting to lure him back. "Surely you miss the days when you were at my side with your brother? Don't you miss us? Think of all you could have if you came to us, think of what you could give your children."

"I have much to give my children when the time comes and it doesn't include the dark path. I do miss my brother but not the person he is now. I have my own family. Now, I've given you my final answer and I don't intend to discuss it further with you so you'll have to excuse us." Alex stood but the guards blocked the door.

"You'll stay for the foreseeable future. You have to give me a chance to make my case."

"You made it. You made it fifteen years ago. I'm not interested. You can't force me and you know it."

George grabbed Lee's arm and yanked her to him. "But I can do all sorts of *unpleasant* things to your bride here to make you change your mind."

Lee sent a bolt of heat through her arm and he let go with a howl of pain. She watched as blisters began to rise on his palm.

"Bitch," he hissed and she sent out a spell to tighten his vocal cords, momentarily cutting off speech.

Alex laughed. "If you expected a weak little tree-hugger you thought wrong."

Lee saw her opening. "Angra, why are you lowering yourself to work with these fools?" she purred.

He looked at her, eyes narrowed. There was so much beauty in his savage face, beauty and insanity.

"Angra?" Alex's grandfather said and backed up a step. "You said you were Damian Cole."

Lee cocked her head and smiled. "Do you really think a mage as powerful as Angra would tell you his real name? You *all* keep your secrets, don't you? After all, I doubt you've told him that you plan to kill him when you'd gotten what you wanted from him." She smirked. "Then again, I don't think that he's the one that will end up dead. You might be powerful, Mr. Carter, but Angra is a mage who was once a god. But you know the name, don't you? I can see your fear," she taunted.

Using the tension between the mages to her advantage she slipped back inside of Angra and planted a small spell that would grow exponentially until it essentially ground him into nothingness. His cells would unravel, slowly at first, and then the spell would gain speed and power until he simply ceased to exist. It was a bad spell, one she would normally never use but she considered it self-defense. He'd tried to hurt them many times, had killed her great-aunt and was planning to try and corrupt her magic and take her will. Since he was the strongest of them, if she could take him out she knew they had a better chance of defeating the others and getting out.

She slipped out and felt Aidan's satisfaction. He knew where they were and had given the information to the families looking for them.

She clasped hands with Alex and unleashed her power as he did his own. They created a spell, meshing their magic and casting a sphere of protection around themselves. Nothing could get in, as his brother and grandfather found out when they tried to cast in their direction.

But it was too late for them anyway as Angra was building up a death spell aimed at the other dark mages. "You think you can kill me? You think you puny little magicians can hold away the thing that I want most? I AM A GOD OF BLOOD AND DEATH AND I WILL EAT YOUR SOULS!" he roared and thrust a spell at Alex's brother so fast he couldn't block it. Peter looked up in surprise and a trickle of blood flowed from his ears as he fell to the ground as if he were a puppet whose strings had been cut.

As Angra was pulling the power of the fallen mage into himself, Alex's grandfather howled in his rage and thrust an energy bolt at Angra to fell him. It glanced off the dark mage's shoulder and he turned, eyes full of fury and madness, and thrust his power at George Carter. Angra's power began to waver as Lee's spell began to take root. The two men were more evenly matched as Angra's power began to dim.

Lee and Alex cast their power out into the hallway, pushing the walls protecting them outward as they moved. She felt Aidan send his power through their bond and it centered her.

The hall echoed with the chanting of spellcasting and the electric hum of great power as the two mages hurled their magic back and forth. Alex stepped just behind his grandfather and stopped.

"You will let us leave, grandfather, or face the consequences. You have violated the rules of the Accord and will have to face judgment. If you continue on, if you survive this battle with Angra, that is, you know the only penalty will be death. There will be nothing left to rule when all of your territory is reclaimed and redistributed," Alex said, a soft wind blowing about the two of them as their power ebbed and flowed like the tide.

George snarled as he continued his battle with Angra but wavered a moment as he sent out a white bolt of energy at Lee and Alex. It was absorbed into the sphere, Lee concentrated and converted it, making their protection even stronger.

"I will make you mine, witch!" Angra shouted and attempted to cast himself into Lee's power, spreading his darkness over her. The sphere protected them for the most part but Lee had to fight down her panic when his oily power touched her own.

Focus, my love. He is not as powerful as you are. Do not fear, she heard Aidan whisper through the link.

She cast deep into herself and bent his power back upon itself and saw her spell working, the magic eating away at him, destroying him like locusts in a field. It rolled over him and she shunned his touch, sending it back to him, accelerating the spell until he fell to his knees and then toppled forward, growing fainter and more insubstantial with each moment.

Lee turned to George, who was leaning against a wall, ashen-faced and drained of power, looking down at Peter's still body. He'd been substantially weakened by Angra's attacks. She cast into his mind and whispered, *You see what I did to Angra, I can do it to you in the blink of an eye.*

He faltered as he looked down and watched Angra cry out one last time before he dissolved into nothingness. He took a step back and motioned to the guards. "Let them go." He looked back toward Alex and Lee. "You've won today, boy. Your witch bride is strong and you have grown in power as well. Together you are a force to be reckoned with. But this isn't over and you know it. Your place is here at my side."

Alex snorted and they walked up the stairs and into the hallway of a large home where they literally bumped into assorted family members that had just arrived to help them.

"Son, are you well?" Giles asked Alex, looking at him carefully.

"Yes. But he's broken the Accord, the families will have to sit in judgment."

Giles got a wicked gleam in his eye. "He's been walking fine lines for years but kidnapping and attempted coercion into the dark path, he's in for it and I suspect that this house will be part of our holdings very soon." He and the other males from his part of the family went belowstairs to intercept George.

But Alex's grandfather didn't get to where he was by simply giving up, he had joined his power with the other dark wizards who were his guards and they rose up out of the basement on a wave of power.

Lee shoved her father out of the way and threw up a defensive shield and began to weave a spell that would paralyze George. While she did that, Alex and his father hit the older man back twice as hard. Power arced off the walls as the spells bounced off shields, Lee was knocked down by one of the defensive spells that had gotten through her shield when she attempted to cast her own spell out.

"*Maman!*" Lee yelled as her mother stepped next to her and grasped her hand.

"Let's join our power and we'll take this *chien mauvais* and send him to hell where he belongs," she said confidently.

Lee wanted to laugh at her mother calling the old powerful wizard an evil dog but she gave a small smile instead and channeled her mother's power into her own and sent out the spell of paralysis as well as a spell to freeze his vocal chords.

It hit him square in the chest and he blinked in shock, eyes wide and face reddening with fury as he fell over backwards, unable to move or speak. Alex's uncles and father rushed over to his grandfather and chanted a binding spell and took over from there. The other wizards helping Alex's grandfather had been drained and were too weak to put up a fight as a group of men came into the house and took them all away.

Lee took in the men, who all looked as if they could be politicians and lawyers. Despite the fact that they all looked like professional men, she could feel their power, both as individual men of magic and as a unit, flow around them, touching everything in their wake. "Who are they?" Lee asked Alex as she watched them wield their magic to bind the remaining dark mages.

"Keepers of the Accord. Sort of like the wizard cops. My grandfather broke the rules by trying to coerce me. We're free to practice the dark path but we can only do it by free choice. He attempted to kill other wizards in other than self-defense. He'll be tried and my guess is that they'll either kill him or drain him of his power and give his holdings to the injured family. In this case, that would be us. Since I don't want it, I'll give them to my father. If that's okay with you," he added.

"More than okay," she said as she let him hug her and kiss the top of her head.

Her mother pulled Lee into her arms. "Sweetheart, I can smell the power on you. You saved yourself and your husband today. You should be proud."

"I used my magic to kill Angra," Lee whispered.

Marie sighed and hugged her more tightly. "Yes, you did. How does it feel?"

"Awful and good at the same time. I had to do it or he wouldn't have stopped coming at us but..."

"Using such magics is bad for you, yes? Makes you feel tainted?"

She nodded and her mother kissed her forehead. "Good. It's not supposed to feel okay, you're supposed to feel bad. Killing is never anything that should be done lightly or without conscience."

"It wasn't your fault, Lee, you had to do it," Alex said quietly, angry with Lee's mother for not trying to make Lee feel better.

"It was my fault, I'm the one who killed him. But I'd do it again because I had no real choice."

He helped them all outside and into the cars in the long drive.

Lee's mother hugged her tight and then when she'd gotten into the car said quietly to Alex, "You're angry that I didn't brush away Lee's anguish over killing the dark mage."

"Yes! She did what she had to do. That basement was filled with wizards, she used that to turn them against each other to fight amongst themselves, wearing them down. But he was still strong, if she hadn't have planted that spell, we might not have gotten out."

"I know that. She's a smart woman, a powerful witch. But she's got to balance that, respect her power. She is my child, Alex, and as such it's my job to help her understand the consequences of being so powerful that she can kill with a few words. It's a big responsibility. She can handle it, I know my child. But she should never take killing lightly." She kissed Alex's cheek and closed the car door.

As they'd been about an hour outside of Chicago, they dropped Lee's family at the airport to fly back home and then continued back to Alex's condo where Aidan was waiting for them.

Epilogue
Six months later

Lee screamed out as the tongue flicking over her swollen clit drove her to orgasm. Alex chuckled and flashed a satisfied look at Aidan, who had just come deep in Lee's throat and had his own satisfied look on his face.

She moved up and each man moved so that she was in between them, caressed by each. She casually stroked each cock in a spare fist and they slipped into a nap.

Lee slipped into a dream state where she watched the busy evening street scene through the glassed walls of a hotel lobby. She looked down at her lap and saw that her hands were clenched together, but they weren't her hands, they were Em's. Em's amethyst and silver ring sat on her lovely long finger. Through Em's eyes, she looked up and saw an elderly woman walk in. She waved a hello and stood up.

"Hello, Mrs. Belton, it's lovely to see you," Em said, clasping hands with the other woman.

"You too, dear. I hope you're hungry, the restaurant is only a few blocks away and we can talk about the books while we eat," the woman said with a smile.

They walked out onto the sidewalk. "London is such a lovely city. I can't believe I don't—" Before she could finish her sentence she was nearly knocked over by a tall caramel-haired man.

"Oh, pardon me," the man said as he helped her back upright.

Em's eyes locked with his and a roar filled her ears…

Lee sat up, stunned. Both men looked at her, concern on their faces.

"I need to call Em!" she said and scrambled over Alex to grab the phone.

The End